Junah at the
End of the World

Junah at the End of the World

a novel

Dan Leach

HUB CITY PRESS
SPARTANBURG, SC

Copyright © 2025
Dan Leach

Cover Design: Kate McMullen and Meg Reid
Book Design: Kate McMullen

Executive Director, Publisher: Meg Reid
Managing Editor: Kate McMullen
Marketing Assistant: Julie Jarema
Editor: Katherine Webb-Hehn
Copy editor: Stephanie Trott

Library of Congress Cataloging-in-Publication Data

Names: Leach, Dan, 1985- author.
Title: Junah at the end of the world : a novel / Dan Leach.
Description: Spartanburg, SC : Hub City Press, 2025.
Identifiers: LCCN 2025000434
ISBN 9798885740494 (trade paperback)
ISBN 9798885740555 (epub)
Subjects: LCGFT: Novels.
Classification: LCC PS3612.E212755 J86 2025
DDC 813/.6--dc23/eng/20250117
LC record available at https://lccn.loc.gov/2025000434

First Edition | Printed in the USA

HUB CITY PRESS
186 W. Main Street
Spartanburg, SC 29306
864.577.9349 | www.hubcity.org

To the true survivors of the apocalypse—
Reagan, Eisley, Beckett, and Marlow

September 1999

W<small>HEN</small> I <small>STEPPED</small> into Miss Meechum's class for the first day of sixth grade, there were shoeboxes on all the desks and a message on the chalkboard that read: <small>THE END OF THE WORLD IS HERE.</small> Having arrived early, I stood alone in that sunlit room smelling of old books and bleach, and I repeated those strange words, as if incantation would surface the secret connection between doomsday and shoeboxes. I was twelve, an age where it is still possible to be moved by the mystery of endings.

When the rest of the kids arrived, everyone sat down at their desks, and Miss Meechum smiled her first-day-back smile. She asked about our summers. We told her we stayed home. Eventually, someone inquired about the shoeboxes, at which point Miss Meechum gestured toward the chalkboard and said, "Raise your hand if you've heard about Y2K."

My hand was among the raised. Secretly, though, I was short on logistics. I knew Y2K had something to do with computers, something to do with banks, and possibly something to do with God. The connections were stated but nebulous. Starting in the spring of that year, there was much talk about when the world was ending, but far less on why.

Like most twelve-year-olds, I had composed my existential stance in relation to my parents, who were divorced but still on speaking terms, especially where my education was concerned. I lived in Greenville with my mother, who was an emergency room nurse with a deep love for Christ. She had spent the summer filling our garage with canned food, bottled water, and other cataclysmic essentials. Dinner talk now included hypothetical apocalyptic scenarios. Night prayers waltzed around the possibility of a rapture.

"I'm not saying something will happen," my mother said. "I'm saying something *could* happen."

My father, a hospital administrator and noncommittal theist, played an affable skeptic but offered little in the way of assurance. "We should be fine" was the closest he came to faith in the future, and I never liked the way his voice wavered on the word "should."

Now here was sweet Miss Meechum, on our first day back from summer, explaining to us that the world was approaching ruin, yet doing so with blue eyes that said, "Even still, everything will be okay." The ambiguity of the adult realm made you dizzy with fear but also wonder. It was unsettling but better (by far) than the tired normal.

"It's the zeros," Miss Meechum continued. "Our computers could handle 1998, and they could handle 1999. But when 2000 rolls around, when those zeros arrive—crash!"

The word "crash" conjured images of skyscrapers imploding, their grey bases reduced to dust as if blasted by dynamite, their structures crumbling downward to join the citywide cloud of steel and glass and concrete. I envisioned all the countries of all the continents, clear down to Antarctica, crumbling simultaneously into fractured, worthless wastelands, all because a computer couldn't carry an extra zero. A whole world, hardly mine: gone.

My imagination tended toward the extreme, but most of Miss Meechum's prophecies were couched in the interrogative, leaving you to decide at what speed and in what manner oblivion would occur.

"What do you suppose will happen?" she asked, still blue-eyed and smiling. "When the power plants black out? When the airports no longer have radar? What about when banks lose their passwords and federal governments lose their nuclear codes?"

A girl in the front of the room raised her hand. She had pigtails the color of lemonade and braces that gave her words a wet, crackling quality. She was from California and had the posture of a natural genius long-bored with mediocrity.

"That's not going to happen," the girl said. "It's true there was a problem with the numbers, but they've fixed it. The transition into the new millennium will be fine. Watch the news."

Miss Meechum laughed. The girl from California glared.

"The news has one purpose," said Miss Meechum. "The sedation of the masses."

The girl's mouth let out a viciously moist click, a sound I took to mean, "This is nonsense. This is lunacy. I need out of Carolina and back home to California." Miss Meechum continued unfazed.

"Expect the best," she said. "Prepare for the worst."

Which brought us to the shoeboxes. Miss Meechum picked one up and held it out in front of her the way a parent might hold a swaddled infant.

"What is this?" she said, gently hefting the object.

"A shoebox," answered a brown-haired boy in the middle row.

"Wrong," said Miss Meechum. "This is a time capsule."

We all looked at the boxes on our desks as if, because of Miss Meechum's smile, they were no longer boxes at all. Mine was bright red with NIKE in white letters and, beneath that, the word CHALLENGER I opened it up and peeked inside. It was clean and empty. It smelled like tangerines.

"Here is your assignment," said Miss Meechum. "For the next four months, we're going to fill these with things that tell what it was like to be alive in Carolina at the end of the world. Your capsule will tell your story."

"Let me guess," said the girl from California. "After we fill them up, we're going to bury them."

Miss Meechum nodded. The girl crackled.

"It would be tempting," Miss Meechum continued, "to view this assignment as an act of preservation. But let me offer an alternative perspective. This is not just a way to protect the past. It's a chance to connect with the future."

"But if the world is ending," said the girl. "Who will be here to find them?"

It was a strange look on Miss Meechum's face— not anger but not grace, not sadness but not joy, and nothing so readable as pity—when she looked down on the girl and said, "Maybe somebody. Maybe nobody. You tell me."

My father found the assignment morbid. My mother thought it was wonderful. They had been divorced since I was seven, and since he lived in a house across town, it was easy to eavesdrop on their land-line dialogues. I sat in the dark of my bedroom and listened, hoping for the same dumb thing I always hoped for when I eavedropped. That some minor detail of my life would serve as the occasion for the two of them to remember how much they used to love each other. That my father would say "I'm sorry" for whatever it was that compelled him to leave. That my mother would say "You're forgiven" and "Come home." That I would reveal my presence with an explosion of laughter and ask the both of them, "What the hell took you two so long?"

Since their stated reason for separating was "We stopped making each other happy," and since recovering misplaced happiness seemed (to me) a fairly minor quest, I passed the time in the subjunctive mood, always imagining what could be but never presupposing what would be. This kind of waiting is arduous work, but it is also the perfect preparation for facing a potential apocalypse, since it teaches you how to expect everything and nothing at the same time.

"Kids have enough to worry about," my father said. "Why's a teacher adding death to the mix?"

"We're Christians," my mother said. "Death is the mix."

"*You* are a Christian," he said. "Junah's like me—a seeker. Plus, he's twelve. You know what I thought about when I was twelve? The Green Bay Packers, that's what. Vince Lombardi, Fuzzy Thurston. That and the Lone Ranger."

"Junah's not like you at all. He's a thinker."

"I'm not opposed to thinking," my father said. "But what's wrong with age-appropriate fixations?"

At this, my mother laughed her large-hearted, melodious laugh.

"What would those entail?" she said.

"I don't know," my father said. "Sports. Music. Girls."

Again I heard my mother's wonderful laughter, after which she whispered either "That sure sounds like fun," or "You don't know your son."

The next clear line belonged to my father, who said, "This thing has everyone out of their right mind."

"Don't pretend you know what's going to happen," my mother said. "None of us do."

A long silence followed this, one that said (on my father's end), "I can't talk about this anymore," and one that said (on my mother's end), "How could we talk about anything else?" They had been arguing about the millennium since spring and had arrived at the same impasse that marked so many of their other, smaller arguments, mainly, "There's no way to know who's right, so I guess we'll have to wait and see."

Not long after this silence, they said goodnight and hung up. I got back in bed and fell asleep thinking about the assignment and how it felt like I had been practicing my whole life to arrive at this one work of curation. My mother had referred to me as a thinker, but that was misleading. More accurately, I was a rememberer and a nostalgia junky, a lonely gatherer of fragments with a mind wired in reverse.

Where most kids my age looked forward, I gazed back. For as long as I had been cognizant of thought, every piece of my past that should have faded—every face, every song, every leaf of every tree in the woods behind our house—it all got brighter in time. This is why I froze up when faced with questions about what I wanted for dinner, or what I planned to do on the coming weekend, or (worst of all) what I might become if the world did not end. Because the future always bored me. Because I would much rather roam the past for something impossibly obscure, say, the color of the scales on the mermaid that was tattooed on the forearm of the ex-Navy alcoholic who delivered mail to our home for several months in the fall of 1992. There it is: deep turquoise with faint dabs of violet.

Miss Meechum said our capsules needed to tell a story, but my mind falls in fragments, not narrative. Let's begin here, then: with a pair of photographs.

First photograph: my family (before the divorce). Here are the three of us standing in front of our house on Christmas morning. We have come out onto the lawn in our pajamas—my father, my mother, and me—in order to watch the first flakes of snow drifting down from the sky. My parents are looking at me, and I am looking up, and everyone is smiling, there in the yard, by the Japanese maple whose wine-red leaves are jeweled with frost. If you are wondering why we look surprised, it's because it never snows in Carolina. If you are wondering why we look as happy as we have ever been, it's because we are. Take note, survivor: these are my people.

Second photograph: The Pipe. I thought about giving you a picture of my room, but since I spent more time in The Pipe than in my room, and since (according to Miss Meechum) the goal here was for you to understand something about me, this seemed like the better contribution. The Pipe was an old drainage tube in the woods behind our house. It had not drained anything for as long as we had lived there, since the creeks at either end were dried up, but it appeared at the base of a leafy hill like the entrance to some forgotten cave. You could enter The Pipe at one end and, with a slight stoop, walk the fifty feet of concrete tunnel (the middle of which was cool and dark) then emerge into the light on the other side of the hill. When I was young, it hosted fantasy. It was the dungeon where the princess was trapped. It was the haunted caverns where the pirate king stored his treasure. As I got older, it became a place to hide. Sometimes I was hiding from the heat of a summer day. Sometimes I was hiding from the world. If there is anything to be gleaned from a person's preferred geography, hold this one close.

What life with its sad kinetics could learn from the photograph. Everything still long enough to be witnessed. Everyone at peace with wherever they've been fixed. Life scrambles. It squirms. But a photograph you can hold.

The next day, Miss Meechum had us write a letter of introduction to place in the time capsule. Mine was brief, including only my name (Junah, after my uncle), my age (twelve), and my reason for composing the capsule (which was not only to appease Miss Meechum but also to see what I could find in my impressions of this place). I finished the letter in three sentences, neatly folded the paper into a snug triangle, and placed it in the capsule alongside the photographs.

Three sentences felt sufficient, especially for an introduction, but when Miss Meechum read it, she said it was "criminally concise" and "wildly impersonal."

"All logistics," she said. "No heart."

"Does this mean I have to write a new letter?"

"Yes," she said. "This time, leave some blood on the page. Give me one paragraph on your deep wounds and another paragraph on your deep loves. Due tomorrow, no excuses."

After school that day, I went to The Pipe. No one was there, and it was quiet, and the way the light fell at both ends made it feel natural to put pencil to paper and lay one word in front of the next. I wrote, beginning with my deep wounds. How I was shorter than everyone else (much shorter) and how my size brought on many years of verbal and physical abuse. I wrote about how I suffered from a speech impediment (a bad one) and how this handicap caused me to hate myself and doubt my language. I wrote about how lonely it feels to grow up in the South as an only child with a body that wouldn't grow and a voice that doesn't work, and how sometimes this particular constellation of weirdness made me want to kill myself. The paragraph ran for three pages (front and back). I had no idea my wounds were so generative.

The paragraph on my deep loves was longer, as it included all the books I loved, and all the songs I loved, and all the things I loved about living where I did, which were too many things to count. I wrote about my mother, an emergency room nurse who caught fire for Christ when I was two. I wrote about my father, a bored middle-manager with a deep need for Clemson football. The Saturdays we used to dress up in orange and drive down to Death Valley, and the Sundays we used to wake up early to worship at the Methodist church down the road. I told about their divorce, and about my continued hope in their coming back together. I told about The Pipe, and about the half-acre yard with the Japanese maple out front, and about the pool down the street we used to walk to in the summer. This paragraph ran for six pages, but it could have easily gone on forever.

The next day, I showed the new letter to Miss Meechum, and she said, "Finally—blood."

After Miss Meechum's class was Coach Mac, who taught us History. Here are Coach's first words from the first day of school: "You are not a child anymore, so don't act like one!"

The proximate apparatus supported Coach Mac's thesis. Behind the school, instead of a sandbox and a playground, there was a football field and a track. In the hallways, instead of brightly colored murals and cubby boxes, there were gray walls and steel lockers. The desks you sat in, the books they gave you, even the food they served for lunch—all of it was heavier, with sharper edges. All of it was screaming, "You are here to become an adult!"

It was a dizzying thing to be told, in one breath, that the world was ending, and in the next breath that you needed to grow up just in time to die. If middle school taught me anything, it was this: make peace with contradiction.

It was said that Coach Mac lived alone in a trailer on the edge of town because his wife had left him for a lawyer down in Charleston.

"That's why he's so mean," said one girl. "That's why he's so sad."

Coach Mac did not look sad to me. After school let out, when the other teachers drove home in their busted-up cars, you could watch Coach Mac climb up on the roof of the school, where he would lift weights and drink beer. He had a busted-up radio that played classic rock and a little refrigerator to keep his booze cold. There was a group of slackers who said one time they hid in the shrubs and threw rocks at him. They said he appeared at the edge of the roof with a smile on his sweaty face and with a fistful of golf balls. They said he pelted them with the golf balls until they ran away, at which point they heard him scream, "Get lost, shitbirds!"

Long before being tasked with filling a time capsule, I collected such vignettes. They gave me hope.

Before becoming a middle-school English teacher in upstate South Carolina, Coach Mac served two tours in Vietnam, where he did things with napalm that still showed up in his nightmares. Before that, he was a light-heavyweight in north Georgia with a left hook that reminded people of Sonny Liston. He was married twice, both times to a woman named Jody. He grew up in Tennessee but moved to South Carolina because he wanted to be close to the beach. He liked Jack Kerouac, so he became an English teacher, and the school needed a coach, so he became Coach Mac. Favorite beer: Miller Lite. Favorite song: "Who'll Stop the Rain?" by Creedence Clearwater Revival.

"How do you know all this?" asked my father, one night on the phone.

"He told us," I said.

"During class?"

"Sometimes," I said. "And sometimes after."

Among my peers, nothing was less cool than admitting you loved the world enough to feel blue over its ending. You could be grizzled and apocalyptic, such as Sarah Winters, who said, "It's about damn time someone put a stop to this shitshow." Or you could be tranquil and indifferent, such as Matt Sumpter, who said, "We had a good run, but nothing lasts forever." What you couldn't be was enamored, and since no one was more enamored than me, no one was less cool than me. I was not cool but also not sorry. All these wonderful people walking around with their weird secrets and unpublished thoughts—not only did I not want the world to end, I wanted to hold it like a photograph for as long as time would let me.

Me: "Hey, Dad, do you think it's uncool to love the world?"

My father: "Absolutely."

Me: "Why? Because it's ugly and full of death?"

My father: "No. Because no matter how well you love it, the world will always break your heart."

Me: "What then? Become a cynic? I'm only twelve."

My father: "Hell no. Cynicism is cowardly. Better dumb and broken-hearted than spineless and clever."

Me: "You're not leaving me a lot of options here. Either way I come out grifted."

My father: "Welcome to living."

"Keep on writing. Even when it's tough, keep going. To fix your memories in writing is to kick Death in his teeth. Some people say we write because we want to know and be known. What a crock! We write because we want to live forever."
—*Miss Meechum*

"I don't know about all of that. I guess I like the way it feels. You write one word, then another. Before you know it, you have a sentence. It's a thought, but it better be more than a thought. It better be music. You read it out loud, and it makes you smile. All this for free. All this because you can." —Coach Mac

I composed some minor riffs for the capsule, and I faked passion for the teachers, but I never gained a serious affection for writing. What I loved was to look. Look: the Japanese maple has turned popsicle-orange. Look: Miss Meechum has a mole on her neck in the shape of a hammer. Look: there's a plastic solemn Jesus on my mother's dusty dashboard. Writing is okay. I should have been a painter.

After several weeks of adding items to the time capsule, it occurred to me that ours is a project of trust. You are trusting me to include only the most significant objects, objects which, once arranged, will tell you a story. I am trusting you to receive these objects and form certain connections. We are, the both of us, divorced by time and bound up in contingencies.

Take the plastic dashboard Jesus from my mother's van. If you favor sincerity, you might find this relic and intuit that it symbolizes my religious convictions. But if your interpretations tend toward cynicism, you might see this figurine as some kind of critique of commodified spirituality.

Both readings would be wrong. I included the plastic Jesus because of my mother. Before my father left, my mother was casual in her faith. After he was gone, she became a fanatic, though not for institutional religion so much as the person of Jesus Christ. My mother loved Christ so much she viewed believers as His beloved bride, and the world as a temporary situation. "A vapor," she often called it. "A prelude."

She would quote the Apostle Peter, who said believers are "strangers and pilgrims" in this world. She would quote the Apostle Paul, who said believers are "citizens of heaven." This was not mere theology. This was her purpose in this life and her hope for the next one, and if the world was going to end, she intended to see her only child saved before it did.

I wanted to believe, but I could not shake the questions. First and foremost: the scandal of invisibility.

"If Christ loves us," I asked her one night. "Wouldn't He want us to see Him?"

"He does let us see Him," she said. "In the Bible. In our hearts."

"That's not the same. I want to see Him like I see you. I want to talk to Him like we're talking now."

There was a look that came over my mother's face whenever I expressed such doubts. It wasn't a look of disappointment or frustration. In fact, it was almost a look of sympathy, as if she felt sorry that I lacked the imagination to envision a God who was ever-present yet never-visible, ever-speaking yet never-audible. It was the look you would give to a child who is trying his best to solve a math problem, except that, no matter how many times he adds it up, he can never arrive at the correct sum.

"He is out there," she said. "Just because you cannot see Him, it doesn't mean He isn't out there."

I could not help but ask, "Where is out there?"

There was a window by my bed. My mother tapped her fingernail against the glass. "Heaven."

When she was gone, I lay on my side and stared up at the sky, which was no longer the sky. Now it was a window between Jesus's house and mine, between out there and in here.

I asked the window, "You home?" But from the window came nothing. An abundance of blackness. A few stars. And, poking like a baby's head over the tops of the trees, the rounded dome of the moon.

I remembered my mother's fingernail tapping against the glass. I got dressed and went outside. I gathered all the rocks I could find and began throwing them at the sky. I wanted to see His face in the window. Failing that, I wanted to put a crack in the divide between out there and in here. My father was probably right—I was more seeker than believer.

How much of this story will you excavate from a plastic figurine? And if the answer is "None," what will you tell in its place? The longer this assignment continues, the more it occurs to me: this is your story, not mine. I pack and bury the box, but the resurrection is on you.

What is faith like in the future? Back here, you throw rocks, but no one shows. You lay in the darkness of your room and listen to the wind in the trees outside your window. It can get hard to move in your cramped list of possibilities:

1. He didn't open when I knocked, which means He's not real.
2. He didn't open when I knocked, which means He's not home.
3. He didn't open when I knocked, which means He's real and He's home, but after seeing it was me, He decided not to answer.

My mother loved Christ so much she refused to be called a Christian.

"We need a new word," she said to me. "America ruined that one. The people with the most hate in their hearts call themselves Christians. The people who make war on other countries call themselves Christians. The people who love money and power and attention call themselves Christians."

"Are you saying that none of those people actually know God?"

"No," she said. "I'm saying you have to kill a bad word before a good one can take its place."

The assignment requires me to tell you about my place, and I love my place, yet I am weary of pickled riffing about the South. Oh the mountains! Oh the beaches! Oh the green sprawling cities that make the wide avenues of Elsewhere seem lovely as used floss! This is all true, but sometimes I get bored with the truth.

My father once told me that you could learn more about a man from the contents of his pockets than from any story he told you about himself. This is how I will tell you about the place I love, which is

South Carolina. I will empty its pockets for you to sort through.

Straight from the pocket: the other night, right as I was falling asleep, I heard the sound of someone knocking on our door. I answered it, and it was the boy from across the street.

"Follow me!" he said. "I have something to show you!"

I didn't tell my mother I was leaving. I slipped out and followed this boy to a cul-de-sac, where a street-lamp had carved a circle of light onto the rain-slick pavement. In that circle was a lump, grey and still, no bigger than a fist.

"It's a bat," whispered the kid. "And he's dead."

This last fact gave me confidence. I drew closer. The little bones in its wings, his silent pink face: I stared deeply at the place where his eyes should have been. I felt that this was all wrong, and I wanted to bury him.

"Don't touch him," the kid said.

I heard this but bent down anyway and lifted him by his wing into the light. For a moment the wing was a backlit map with veins that ran wild with rivers. There were many odd-shaped countries carved out in tiny bones.

I held him and knew what needed to happen.

"I have to bury him," I said to the kid.

I was going to say more, but before I could—a resurrection, in my own palm. There was the flapping, then the screeching, then the angry mouth swinging around to sink its teeth into my thumb. I released him, but he refused to release me.

After it was over and the bat had flown off, we stood there in the cul-de-sac and stared at the blood leaking out of my hand. I was laughing. The kid was crying. Neither of us could have said why.

Later that night, I woke up from a deep sleep, and my hand was on fire with pain. Because of the darkness of my room, and because of how intense the pain was, I thought the bat had returned and was biting me again. I turned on the lights to calm myself down. I had to say, out loud and more than once, "You are alone here. He is out there." I had to remind myself that I had been let go.

You say, "But hold on, that could have happened anywhere. New York. California. Even Ohio." Maybe. Maybe.

My father: You're odd.

Me: Why's that?

My father: Everyone I know is holding their
        breath to see what happens in December.
        Everyone except you.
Me: I've tried it their way.
My father: And?
Me: It bores me.

More from the pocket: everyone at Northwoods
Middle had decided that, since the world was ending,
you had better fall in love before it did. Except they
refused to call it falling in love. They called it getting
"bit."
  "I saw you holding hands with Brooke. You bit?"
  "Yeah, man. I'm bit."
  "You guys know that new girl from Georgia?"
  "Yeah."
  "She bit me."
  "No way."
  "Yeah, man. She bit me hard."

When I told my mother that half the world was bit
and the other half was biting, she surprised me with
her approval.
  "You've spent your entire life loving the past," she
said. "It wouldn't kill you to try loving a person."

I did love a person—Sadie Hayes. But when I told my mother about it, she said, "Sadie Hayes? Isn't she that scab-eater?"

Calling Sadie a scab-eater was not, technically speaking, pejorative. In fact, my mother could not have offered a more objective observation. At school, Sadie had been seen picking, studying, and consuming her own scabs so habitually, so plainly, so unapologetically, everyone called her Sadie the Scab-eater. I had never actually spoken to Sadie, but I had heard that, when Miss Meechum explained to her that eating scabs was "inappropriate," and that some of the other students had complained, Sadie looked Miss Meechum dead in the eye and said, "I don't care what other people find appropriate."

It wasn't just the scab thing. Sadie's insularity was holistic. Back in elementary school, she had wild auburn hair that she refused to brush. Instead, she wrapped the whole tangled mess of it into some kind of lopsided nest that sat on top of her head with the help of camouflage head-wrap. Back then, which is when I first fell for her, her clothes were mismatched, oversized, sometimes dirty, and often inside out. At recess, when other students played, Sadie read comics; and in class, when other students participated, Sadie slept. Between the scab-eating and the apathy, everyone thought she was gross. But they were wrong.

Sadie was original. She was, as far as I could tell, the only one who was inoculated to the most widespread virus around—the fear of dying unloved.

The summer between fifth and sixth grade, Sadie went full punk, and this moved me. She shaved both sides of her head, leaving a thin strip on top, which she dyed neon green and twisted into spikes using Elmer's Glue. She pierced her lip, both eyebrows, and her septum, all in one night, and all using only a safety pin and a bottle of hydrogen peroxide. Everything she wore was black. The leather bomber jacket and the combat boots from the Army Navy Surplus. The chokers and the studded cuffs. The endless supply of ratty shirts for bands like Bad Brains, Rancid, and The Dead Kennedys.

I was made uncomfortable by my mother's reaction, but I was far from ashamed.

"That's right," I said. "Sadie the Scab-eater."

"There are plenty of other—"

"It's Sadie," I said. "I'm bit."

My mother sighed and changed the subject. For a long time to come, we left the subject changed.

I called my father and asked him about Sadie.

Me: You think it's weird to fall for a girl who eats
    scabs?

Him: I once fell for a girl who ate pig's feet. It
        didn't last, but that's no fault of the pigs.
Me: What's your point? Different strokes for
        different folks?
Him: Not exactly. More like, love's too high a
        thrill for nitpickers.
Me: I like that.
Him: You should. It's the truth.

I asked Coach Mac if he believed in love.

"No," he said. "But I believe in believing. And if you can't shake it, love's a better church than money."

Miss Meechum took the capsules home over the weekend and returned them on Monday all filled with little Post-It notes of feedback. One of mine read, *"More vulnerability!"*

Let's get vulnerable, then: I hated a motherfucker named Rusty Riggins. Whatever large and violent creature you imagine when you hear the name Rusty Riggins, double the size and double the hurt, and what you'll have is Rusty Riggins. Rusty's patented move was the sleeper hold, wherein he would sneak up behind you, lock his arm around your neck, and lift you several inches off the ground so that everyone could see your legs spasm as you tried not to black out. You always blacked out, and, once you did, Rusty would drop you on the ground, steal whatever was in your pockets, and culminate his assault by one final abuse, such as drawing cartoon genitalia on your face in permanent marker, or depositing one of your shoes in a toilet.

In class, Rusty liked to chew the inside of his cheek until it bled. He would let his mouth fill up with blood then smile so as to send a red dribble out of his lips and down his chin. He seemed to think this gesture was necessary to convince us of his psychopathic tendencies, but I found it a bit excessive. His lived life gave no indication of a capacity for kindness.

Rusty had never bullied me, but I didn't mistake this for fortuity. He simply needed more time. I knew this because his victims and I shared certain qualities, mainly being small, quiet, and alone.

More vulnerability: I'm not a bully, but I can be a pretender. Such as the other day, when Miss Meechum said, "This is an assignment where you should give yourself permission to be ambiguous! Even feel free to be esoteric!"

After looking up both "ambiguous" and "esoteric," I found a photograph of my father's house (a Polaroid, no less), and I wrote over the surface of the image, "Absence Is Its Own Kind of Architecture." I showed it to Miss Meechum as if it meant something, and as if I had meant something in writing it. She moaned (no exaggeration) and said, "How literary!"

I was tired of looking words up in the dictionary, so when Coach Mac's class came around, I showed him the Polaroid and asked him if he thought it was "literary." He laughed and said, "It is. But you don't want to be literary. Trust me."

"Why not?"

"Because 'literary' comes from the Latin word 'literanus,' which translates as 'one who farts alone in the bathtub and treasures the ensuing smell'."

Since I have no way of knowing how literary the future is, I have left the photograph here for your consideration. Let's pretend it's as real as the rest of this stuff.

Miss Meechum said that the starting point of any composition is listening, an art in which I was well-practiced. Consider this interaction, which happens (if I am lucky) three to six times a week.

"You're kind of quiet," some kid says to me.

I nod my head, so as to imply, "Correct."

"Why's that?" they ask.

"Speech impediment."

They scrunch their faces, so as to imply, "What the hell did you say?"

I repeat myself, slower, as practiced: "Speech impediment."

Cue the Southern sense of sympathy: "That sucks, man. I'm sorry."

"Don't be," I say. "I like it."

"How come?"

"It means I get to listen."

Do the people of the future baffle you? Humans back here were too absurd to fathom. To wit: the day that Rusty Riggins lined his knuckles with keys and punched everyone who passed him. He hit a sixth-grader at the water fountain so hard that the sixth-grader came up with two broken teeth and mouth full of blood. Rusty slapped him in the cheek and said, "Nice smile."

Later that same day, I heard the prettiest girl in school talking to her friend, who happened to be the second prettiest girl in school. She said, "I'm bit."

Her friend tittered and whispered, "Who?"

The prettiest girl in school clutched her heart and said, "Rusty."

The only person in school that Rusty would not mess with—Sadie Hayes.

Another photograph, this one of me. What do you make of it? It has been said I have a look on my face (natural, not affected) that communicates confusion. My mother describes it as "stunned." My father's word is "lost." One classmate said, "You look like you woke up from a dream, except you're mad at us for having brought you out of it."

I don't know what any of this means, except I have to suffer at least one conversation per day to this effect:

"What?" some kid on the playground, in the neighborhood, et cetera. would say.

"What?" I would respond.

"That's what I'm asking you."

"I know. But what's your question?"

"Your face," the kid would say. "Why's it look like that?"

"I'm fine."

"Are you upset about something?"

"No."

"Are you confused?"

"No."

"Then why do you look like that?"

What I wanted to say was this: "Why are you looking at my face? There's so much to see out here. There's birds and trees and, if you're objectively into faces, there are people who would love the attention. Why me?" What I would actually say was, "I was born with it."

There was a distance back here (sometimes infinite) between the voice that belongs to you and the one that belongs to the world.

Miss Meechum told us to contribute an item that a survivor might find helpful. I thought about leaving you my Swiss Army knife, but instead I went with my sunglasses. One day, when I was five, and when my father still lived with us, I rummaged around in his garage and found these, all massive and black, the kind certain elderly folks wear to block out the sun and all of humanity. They were heavy on my face, and I loved the heaviness. I loved having that big, thick piece of dark between myself and the world. I put them on and, for the next few years, they stayed on. I wear them, even in The Pipe, even after dark.

Take the Swiss Army knife too. You never know.

Take Career Day at Northwoods Middle. Career Day meant much talk from parents who were bankers, contractors, and shop owners. It also meant free floss from the dentist and going outside to climb into the cab of a fire truck. The firemen were large, bearded men who let us play with the sirens, and who gave us red plastic helmets.

When the presentations were over, Coach Mac walked to the chalkboard and wrote, "In one hundred words or more, describe your dream job."

I chewed on the end of my pencil, pretending to think about it, but I already knew what my dream job was. I wanted a job where I was left alone all day with absolutely nothing to do. Since no one would bother me, and since I had nothing to do, I would spend my work days reading books and writing stories and taking long naps in which I dreamed about things I had read in the books and written in the stories. I would never miss a day of work for a job such as this.

I once made the mistake of sharing this dream with my parents. They said reading and writing were "attractive skills" and suggested jobs like college professor and copy editor, both of which were laughable compromises.

In response to Coach Mac's prompt, I wrote: "My dream job is to be the toll taker on a road that dead ends in a ghost town."

Coach held me after class to discuss this take.

"Let's talk about being a toll taker," he said. "What specifically interests you about this job?"

I explained to him that I would only consider positions at toll stations on roads that people no longer used—old mill villages, abandoned highways, half-built bridges, etcetera.

"I don't understand," he said. "What would be the point of being a toll taker if there were no drivers to pass your station?"

"The point would be to get your time back."

"Are you saying that jobs steal your time?"

"Yes."

"Do you think that school steals your time?"

"Yes."

"You want a job where you will do nothing. Is that right?"

"No," I said. "I want a job where I am not compelled to do anything. That way, I can do what I want to do."

"Which is?"

"Remembering, more than anything. But also reading. Maybe some napping if there's time."

Coach Mac looked disturbed by this. I asked him

if he was going to call my home. He said that unless I could think of another response, he felt it was his duty to contact my parents.

"Firefighter," I said. "I could also be a firefighter."

Coach handed me a fresh sheet of paper and requested I write a new paragraph. He left me alone, and I was happy to create for him a palatable fiction.

Jobs That Could Suffice If All Positions For Tolltaker On A Road That Dead Ends In A Ghost Town Are Filled:

1. Night Watchman at a Small-Town Aquarium
2. Backup Janitor at Remote Arctic Station
3. Obscure Painter

My father called me on the phone the other night. He said we needed to talk.

Him: Is Miss Meechum still having you work on those time capsules?

Me: She is.

Him: Is your mother still stockpiling food and talking about the Rapture?

Me: She is.

Him: And what about you? What's your take on all of this?

Me: All of what?

Him: The end. The Apocalypse. The world you
　　　know—boom!—gone up like a cherry
　　　bomb.

Me: I don't know. I love it here. Some nights I
　　　can't sleep because I just lay there and
　　　think about all the cruel and beautiful
　　　things that happened in the day. How
　　　could you want something like that to end?

Him: How about that girl? You talked to her yet?

Me: Not yet.

Him: Why not?

Me: I'm thinking about the options for how to do
　　　it.

Him: It's not enough that you arrange the past,
　　　you have to tinker with the future now
　　　too?

Me: I like to think.

Him: You should try living.

Coach Mac gave me a D on the first paper of the
year, which was a short story told from the point-of-
view of a mole. Here was my pitch: "Intrigued by the
sounds of the world above, an apprehensive young
mole considers leaving the comforts of his home."

When I asked why my story earned such a low

grade, Coach said, "Too much time in the subjunctive mood. You had two-thousand words to get that mole out of its hole, and you didn't. It ended right where it began—in possibility."

"Is there anything I can do to raise my grade?"

"A little dramatic action would bring you up to a C. Throw in an epiphany, you'd be looking at a B."

"What do I need to do to earn an A?"

"Write a story about a wolf."

Do you have a nickname? Because I wore sunglasses all the time, mine was "Shades." There was never any illusion that I wore them to look cool. My peers were absurd, but they were not obtuse. They knew I loved humanity by hiding out from it, beginning with them.

Early one Saturday morning, my mother caught me in The Pipe as I was deciding which of my many gemstones I would put inside the capsule. I had it down between my two favorites: a bright amethyst the size of a small egg, or a smooth little heart-shaped jasper shot through with forest greens and chocolate browns.

"Hey," my mother said. "You're spending a lot of time on that assignment."

I pocketed the amethyst and slipped the jasper into the capsule, under a folded map of my neighborhood that I had drawn using the carpenter pencils that once belonged to my grandfather, the architect. I closed the top of the box and composed a tone of respect, which is something Southern mothers value on par with oxygen.

"Yes ma'am," I said. "But this is school work."

"I don't know," she said. "It feels like you're making it into something more."

"Like an obsession?"

"Exactly."

"What is your concern?"

"I know how you are," she said. "And I don't want you to lose yourself in making this thing, okay?"

I said, "No, ma'am," and my mother left me alone, at which point, I emptied the contents of my capsule onto the cool pavement of The Pipe and began, as I had so many times before, arranging and rearranging all of the items, in order to see how each new arrangement unearthed a different story. I would do this work all day. I would do this work until it got dark, at which point I would go home, eat dinner, and lay in my bed so as to happily do the same work all over again: break, build, arrange, repeat.

My mother had said, "I know how you are." She was not wrong. There is nothing I would rather have done than surrender every last ounce of myself to the act of composition.

Following the mole debacle, I wrote another short-story for Coach Mac. This one was told from the point-of-view of a famished wolf. While hunting one day, the wolf spots what appears to be a young deer. Overcome with appetite, he tracks this young deer through many forests and across many rivers. He tracks it high into the mountains and, eventually, down into a cave. When he gets to the bottom of the cave, however, there is no deer. Just a mysterious pool of black water in which he sees his reflection. "Go home," the wolf in the water tells him. "You've been hungry for yourself." Whereas the story about the mole took me three days to write, this one took thirty minutes, and I hated it so much I actually felt embarrassed when I gave it to Coach Mac. He returned it the next day, though. It earned an A-plus.

"A speaker who commits," he said. "That's the move."

When I told Miss Meechum that Coach Mac compared literary writing with farting alone in the bathtub, I expected some kind of rebuttal. Instead, she shrugged and said, "Who doesn't fart in the bathtub?"

School did not encourage thought— it intruded upon it. Even recess was a long run of short interruptions. There I was, hiding behind my sunglasses and minding my own business, watching a caterpillar chew loops through a maple leaf, or drawing a map in the dirt, or (recently) working on the assignment, when— boom!—a goon with glib takes would materialize. This was yesterday (and almost everyday).

"Hey, man," said a voice. "You bit?"

I was by myself on the blacktop to work on my capsule. I looked up from the box and saw it was one of those kids who had been held back several times. This meant he was taller and heavier than everyone else but also that he spoke with a kind of confidence, as if to imply, "I've lived more life than you, so listen up and I'll tell you the score." He smelled like old hamburgers.

"No," I said. "I'm not bit."

He said, "You're that kid who talks weird, aren't you?"

"Nope," I said, not bothering to look up from my rocks. "That's someone else."

"If you're not bit, you got to get bit," he said.

"There's only a few months left. After that—*boom!* Game over."

"Okay."

After this, I continued working in my capsule as I would have if I were alone, while he continued standing over me breathing through his mouth. Your best strategy with such kids is to affirm whatever they propose (regardless of your true feelings), refuse to look them in the face, and let a long spell of awkward silence eventually usher them off. Southerners crave conversations with steady rhythms, so this tactic enjoys a high success rate. But this kid defied the odds and stuck around, very Northern in his capacity for silence.

After a minute of nothing, he kicked the box hard enough to send half its contents spilling out on the pavement, then he spit in the dirt not far from my shoes. He must have drawn closer because the smell of hamburgers filled my nostrils.

"Fuck that assignment!" he said. "It's love, man! Love or nothing!"

I began to regather the contents of my capsule. The heavier items, such as the plastic dashboard Jesus and the Swiss Army knife, had not gone far, but anything made of paper was being carried off by the wind. I wanted to chase after them and actually experienced a mild pain in my chest as I watched them drift farther and farther away. But for some reason, I did not move. I stood up and looked this boy directly in his dirt-brown eyes. (I say "directly," though I had my sunglasses in place for protection.)

"Who loves you?" I said.

On hearing this, he stared at me and said nothing. We stood like that for half a minute, just breathing on one another and waiting for something to happen. Then he smashed his greasy palm into the side of my face and mumbled something I couldn't make out, walking away and leaving me alone on the blacktop.

Whatever the wind could carry out of my capsule and into the world, it had. I saw the scraps and the pages and the drawings that were once so carefully fixed inside my capsule, only now they were spread out across the playground, some skittering into the woods at the south end, some airborne and floating toward the road that curled around the front of the school. What it felt like, watching these pieces that belonged inside the capsule be carried off into nowhere, was a small but felt kind of death.

I was scrambling around the playground, recovering whatever I could, when Miss Meechum found me. She told me it was time to go inside, that the rest of the class was waiting. I explained to her what had happened and insisted that I could not come back until I had brought back everything that had been lost. What she said, as she took my hand and led me back into the building, was this: "Those are other parts to other stories. Whatever's left belongs to this one."

Where the validity of love was concerned: I did not actually require an explanation. One look at Sadie, and I knew that we weren't making too much of love. We were making too little.

Here is the reason I did not ask Sadie Hayes to be my girlfriend, which is the same reason I did not punch Rusty Riggins in his nose or ask the Holy Ghost into my heart: because as long as you keep reality at a distance, you can hold it like a photograph, and it will, if you let it, feel more luminous than life itself.

Maybe this is why I feel so close to you: because of this distance between us that will never be closed. We are together all the time, yet I will never know your name.

I showed my capsule to Miss Meechum, who said, "Keep going. Only weirder. And more disconnected. Like the world, you know?"

I showed my capsule to Coach Mac, who said: "Too many fragments, not enough connections. Jesus, Rusty Riggins, all this stuff about getting bit. What you need is a bit of cohesion. The perfect stories tie everything together."

I thanked him, took up my capsule, and went on my way, more clear than ever on the need for fragments. Perfection? I liked the broken, reaching stuff.

I thought about telling Sadie Hayes that I loved her. I tried to use the end of the world as a catalyst for confidence. It worked until I saw her, at which point my already-broken voice became a pure failure. I continued to pray. Courage, too, detonates on its own terms.

The question of geography is a hard one to duck. That is: is all of this Southern, or merely human? You will have to conduct your own research where this issue is concerned. I am bored with categories, plus the farthest I've been is Virginia.

In Science today, Mr. Welsh explained that eyes are not windows. They are actually tiny cameras. Light enters through the cornea then passes through the lense. After that, the rods configure form and shape, leaving the cones to sort out texture and color. Things get tricky when light reaches the retina. I could not pretend to understand it. Something about light being refracted and inverted. Something about a conversion that turns perceived images into electric signals so as to be relayed to the brain through the optic nerve. I was too grossed out to pursue further research, but a basic takeaway is this—as with photographs, something gets lost in the translation of reality into image. By the time your eye converts light into form, the reality you're trying to capture has already moved forward in time and space. Maybe it was okay that I couldn't see God. Maybe no one ever has.

Everything not a photograph: still, in your eyes, a photograph. Everything old light, everything behind you by the time you hold it. Like all sad ideas, this one makes me happy.

"Listen," my father told me one night on the phone. "You better talk to that girl before it's too late. You're running out of time."

"I thought you said nothing was going to happen? That Y2K was a hoax?"

"That's not what I'm talking about."

"Then what?"

"You want to know what I'm talking about? Keep doing nothing. Keep thinking."

It happened in Coach Mac's class. During a lesson on wartime literature, he fired up an old projector in order to show us footage of Hiroshima. He turned off the lights, and everyone got quiet, and you felt a low-level magic fill the room like smoke when Coach hit the switch and the grainy, black-and-white images splashed on the empty chalkboard. I looked across the room at Sadie, who was sitting up and facing forward, having deemed this particular lesson worthy of her attention.

The film opened with the scientists and construction workers of the Manhattan Project standing around in the desert, where they intended to drop the first atomic bomb.

"They're standing in the Jornada del Muerto," said Coach. "That translates to 'The Journey of Death.'"

Coach paused the film on a frame in which four scientists nervously carried a small box toward a large metal shell. They took small steps and were clearly terrified at the idea of dropping it. They growled sadly at each other like, "Do you have it? Do you?"

"Inside that box is the atomic core," said Coach. "Pure plutonium. No bigger than an orange, but wait until you see what it can do."

Coach started to hit play but stopped himself. He looked out over the class, half of which was asleep, and for some reason, his eyes stopped on me. As if speaking directly to me, he said, "They interviewed one of those scientists who carried the box. He said he could feel the core. He said it felt warm. Like a live rabbit."

I nodded and pretended to take this down in my notes.

When the moment came for the bomb to be dropped, Coach said, "Here it comes. If you're squeamish, cover your eyes."

I was squeamish, but I kept my eyes open. I watched the bomb hit the earth, and the earth turn to flaming dust that ascended in a weirdly beautiful cloud, and as the narrator said, "I looked up at the heavens that day and saw that they were boiling," I looked at the bombed surface, then at Sadie, then back at the surface, then back at Sadie. I was done thinking.

That day at the bus stop, with a sky full of clouds and the air starting to feel like autumn, I dusted off my sunglasses and walked up to Sadie Hayes. I said,

"Hey, Sadie, do you want to go for a walk?"

She was standing at the bus stop, looking like she always looked, which was part-sad and part-angry and part–wishing-there-was-somewhere-else-to-be.

She wore massive red headphones, and though I was standing five feet back, I could hear what sounded like angry people using power tools to destroy something valuable. I stood in front of her and waited for an answer, although it was clear she had not heard the question.

I tapped my ears and mouthed, "Take those off."

To my surprise, she did take them off, and I started to repeat my question, but before I could get it out, she grabbed me by the collar of my shirt, yanked me toward her, and put the headphones on me. Those power tools filled my ears, almost to the point of pain, and the singer was screaming something about walking the streets alone at night, but I stood right where I was, and I looked into Sadie's eyes, and I saw her mouth as she said, "Listen."

I listened but didn't get it. I didn't get why they were angry, or why they were destroying whatever they were destroying. I just knew that, like Sadie, it was not a lie.

The song ended abruptly, and when it did, Sadie snatched the headphones, slipped them on, and boarded her bus. As the bus pulled away, I searched for her face in the long line of dirty windows, but if she was up there, I failed to locate her.

With the bus gone, and the school empty, I started the long walk home. I was humming the song she had shared with me and wondering if the dizzy feeling in my head was what everyone meant when they used the word love. I was halfway to my neighborhood before it hit me—she never answered my question.

I told my mother about the incident at the bus stop.

"Hold on," she said. "Is this still that girl who eats scabs?"

I told her it was, but that this fact had no relevance in this situation.

"Trust me," she said. "You do not want Sadie Hayes for a girlfriend. I've seen that girl. She's crazy."

I told her the truth: there was no one else. Not at school, not at church, and not anywhere else on the planet. When she told me to move on, I reminded her that, due to the impending apocalypse, there was no time to compose a new affection.

"Then here's the next step," she said. "You have to write a note. Nothing fancy. 'Would you like to be my girlfriend?' should suffice. Below this, draw two boxes. One that says 'YES' and one that says 'NO.' Do not ever draw a box for 'MAYBE.' Sign it with your first name, in cursive if possible. But keep it short, okay?"

These were simple instructions with a firm basis in logic. I went back to my room, took up my pen, and wrote the first of what would become thirteen pages (front-and-back). It began, *"Dear Sadie, We don't know each other, and that might seem like a problem, but lately I've been thinking, is it possible for anyone to know someone else? Truly, I mean."*

The next day at school, I gave the note to Billy Beale, who was the closest thing I had to a friend. Billy agreed to deliver it to Sadie. Everything I had went into that note. I knew the genre called for brevity, but if this note was my one chance to show Sadie who I was, I wanted to put as much of myself into the note as possible. I wanted to make it so that if she checked no, she would be rejecting all of me, and if she checked yes, she would be accepting all of me. In this one scenario, I dreamt of fullness, not compression.

Some long-feeling days went by with no response from Sadie.

I asked Billy if he delivered the note.

"I did," he said. "And it looks like even scab eaters are out of your league."

My mother: Look at you.

Me: What?

My mother: You're thinking about the future.
           Probably about that girl with green hair.
Me: How can you tell?
My mother: Your face, mainly. You don't smile
           like you used to.

I asked my father if not getting a response was the same thing as getting a rejection.

"Not necessarily," he said. "Some girls need time."

"Okay," I said. "But what do I do now?"

He laughed at this question like it was the funniest thing he had ever heard.

"Now you get to wait," he said. "Wait and burn."

Here are my old sunglasses. While waiting for Sadie to respond, I found a new pair: turquoise wayfarers from the dollar bin at Goodwill. The kids at school laughed when I wore them, but I cared for their laughter about as much as I cared for the chirping of birds. I was covered, nearly inoculated. I was still watching, and still reaching out to you, but now I had a subquest to keep me busy: waiting for Sadie.

Even Rusty Riggins had a girlfriend. They held hands in the cafeteria. He bit the inside of his cheek and,

when the blood ran down his chin, she was there to
catch it with a folded napkin.

From time to time, I would see Sadie at the bus stop.
I would wave, but it was never clear if she saw me.
I thought about writing another note. My mother
warned against it. She said, "You can do better." I
thought, "Nothing in this world is more boring than
better."

*"Empty your capsule of all clichés, truisms, and
banalities! Having survived the apocalypse, the citizens of the future will be numb to everything that's
not dripping with blood and bottomlessly weird! Put
something in your box that you are sure no one but
you understands. When the future sits down to read
this mystery, know that it will make perfect sense."*
—Miss Meechum

It was the last week of September. With still no word
from Sadie, I called my father and asked if I should
write her another note.

"No," he said.

"Should I talk to her?"

"No."

"How is she going to give me her answer?"

"She already has."

The men in my life formed a kind of pessimists' club. Even before Y2K, they loved to remind you how the world (or, at the very least, America) was coming to an end. They were eulogists of a past I only knew in stories.

"Time was," said Coach Mac. "Children were seen and not heard. Now everything's upside down. Well, let's see what happens when the monkeys run the zoo."

"You know what Nixon said after Watergate?" said Mr. Welsh, my Science teacher. "He said, 'Mistakes were made.' Take that as the death of what made this country great—individual accountability."

"People didn't use to be so damn frail," said my father. "You could disagree with each other without taking offense. You could tell a dirty joke and not get crucified."

Some of my peers resented these critiques, but not me. An old millennium was about to die, and a new one was ready to begin. Anyone could see that these men—"Uncles," we called them—were not hateful. They knew that, even if the world did not end for everyone, it was ending for them.

And yet, in his own way, Coach Mac attempted to encourage us. Consider this riff (the first of many he delivered to our class):

"I know many of you are worried about what will happen in December. Let me assure you, this is not the first time we've dreamed up an apocalypse, and it won't be the last. In 1910, a French astronomer claimed that Haley's Comet would smash into Earth and poison our atmosphere. The greater scientific community dismissed this prediction, but it was too late. When people commit to their anxieties, good luck introducing facts. One woman sold everything she had to buy a lifetime supply of gas masks and bottled oxygen. Another guy lowered himself into a dry well with a gallon of whiskey and a box of anti-comet pills. A religious group in Oklahoma—and I'm not making this up—they tried to sacrifice a virgin. I can see from your faces that this is freaking some of you out, but all I'm trying to say here is that we're going to be okay. It's their job to tell you the world is ending. It's your job to say, 'We'll see.'"

I talked to Billy, who believed the best way to forget Sadie was to get another girl.

"Try Aimee Quinn," he said.

"Why Aimee Quinn?"

"Because," he said. "Aimee could get bit by a rock."

With Aimee Quinn, I kept it shorter: nine pages instead of thirteen. Billy was out sick, so I broke protocol and handed the note directly to Aimee. She smiled when I gave it to her, which seemed an auspicious sign. Unlike Sadie, she immediately began reading the note and replied within the hour. On the ninth and final page there were two boxes, one for 'YES' and one for 'NO.' Aimee had checked the 'NO.'

When I reported this rejection to Billy, he said, "Try Casey Hubbard."

"Why Casey Hubbard?"

"Because Casey Hubbard says yes to everyone."

With Casey Hubbard, I wrote to one page, the last section of which rejected the check-box method in favor of a numbered scale. Below the scale, it read, "*From 1 to 10, with 1 being 'Let's Continue Being Strangers' and 10 being 'I Absolutely Would Love to Be Your Girlfriend,' what are your feelings about me?*" Casey returned the note later the same day. She had drawn an extra notch to the left of 1, over which she wrote and circled 0.

Neither rejection fazed me. I had faked both crushes. After Sadie, you were down to two options: one, unseemly lamentation; two, performative well-being. I lived out option number two.

"Here's another one," said Coach Mac. "In 1499, a mathematician in Germany claimed that the world would end in a great flood. He was a numbers guy, so he provided a specific date for when the water would come. February 20, 1524. People all across Europe marked their calendars and lost their minds. Thousands of folks, and not just Germans, either bought or built boats. There was a nobleman, Count von Iggleheim, who built a three-story ark designed to sail forever down the Rhine. When February 20, 1524 rolled around, a light rain began to fall, and the people in Iggleheim's town formed a mob and demanded seats on his ark. By the end of the day, the rain had stopped, and Iggleheim was stoned to death. Moral of the story—be careful what you wish for."

For a long time there, at the end of September, it was the books and the music and loneliness like a default setting. I woke up lonely, I moved through the day lonely, and at night, if I didn't feel lonely, I asked my mom to take my temperature.

Because of bad television, we think loneliness is feeling alone in a crowded room and wishing someone would look at your face. But that feeling, if anything, is a diminished form of hope. That feeling seeks and usually (in time) finds connection in another. True loneliness is feeling like everyone in the room *is* looking at your face, but even if they looked all night, even if they crossed the room and asked about your favorite book, they still wouldn't understand a single thing about you.

If you can't outrun a thought, you make peace with it. The world was worth looking at (even if it was dying), and there are worse crimes than meeting the end with no girl by your side. I spent my time at The Pipe and was happy. I had you with me.

My mother was worried that I had no friends. She kept asking, "Don't you get lonely?"

I asked her, "What's wrong with being alone?"

"Absolutely nothing," she said.

"Then why is everyone so obsessed with relationships?"

At this my mother laughed.

"Because," she said. "It's good to be around people."

"Why?" I asked.

"Because people can help each other."

"*Help*? That's why everyone is crazy about relationships?"

"That's it."

"Are there no alternatives?"

My mother thought about it, then said, "Christ."

"Yeah, but what does He want from me?"

"A relationship."

Here is a confession you did not need spelled out: I like loneliness. Loneliness is where I feel farthest from the world but closest to you. It's where the past dresses up like the present and dances as long as you'll let it.

Me: The ambiguity is beginning to lose its charm. Tell me straight—is Y2K for real?

My mother: If it is, we will be prepared.

Me: Yes, I've seen the mountain of canned tuna out in the garage. But what if it isn't?

My mother: Do you like tuna fish sandwiches?

Me: I do.

My mother: Then don't worry about it.

"The question is not 'Will the world end in December?'
The question is 'How might you live as if it will?'"
—Miss Meechum

October 1999

HERE IS AN excerpt from an Assyrian clay table (2800 B.C.) that Coach Mac distributed during today's class: "Our earth is degenerate in these later days; there are signs that the world is speedily coming to an end; bribery and corruption are common; children no longer obey their parents; every man wants to write a book and the end of the world is evidently approaching."

Because she could not stop reading the Gospels, my mother left me with many clear memories of Jesus.

My favorite comes from Luke's account. Jesus has just served the Last Supper to His disciples and is praying in a garden when the Roman soldiers arrive to arrest Him. To protect the man he believes to be the Savior of the World, Simon-Peter draws his sword and hacks off the ear of a soldier named Malchus. Jesus picks up the ear, reattaches it to Malchus's head, and says, "No more of this." Peter's crime: reversed. Malchus's ear: restored. Time: reset. Some nights, I actually prayed that, should the worst happen in December, the Lord would throw down such a gracious subversion.

I could not accept everything my mother told me, but I could not stop hoping that most of it was true. Carolina is full of Doubting Thomases. We love the Jesus we see, but we have a hard time believing the One we don't.

"Last one," said Coach Mac. "New England. May 19, 1780. In the middle of the afternoon, the sun stopped shining, and the sky turned black as night. Animals went wild, and everyone in the region thought the end of the world was at hand. Everyone except a legislator named Abraham Davenport. When the rest of the legislature panicked and recommended adjournment, so as to get the hell out and prepare for the apoc-alypse, Davenport said, 'The day of judgment is either approaching, or it is not. If it is not, there is no cause of an adjournment; if it is, I choose to be found doing my duty. I wish therefore that candles may be brought.' Eventually the sun returned, and it was discovered that forest fires were the cause of the darkness. Moral of this one—do your duty. If neces-sary, by candlelight."

By the end of September, my duty had become the assignment. It was dizzying and sometimes depress-ing work, but it encouraged me to envision you, out there, waiting.

Miss Meechum brought in a replica of a Cornell Box to prove a point about absence. In this particular box, the artist had arranged a large rusted key, a double-three domino, and a small cream-colored conch, all set against a torn piece of sheet music.

"Focus on the key," she said. "What associations does that item raise in your mind?"

The girl from California with the lemonade hair and the braces had long since transferred to a differ-ent (read: better) school. Which left the task of thoughtful responses to a girl from Ohio, who also had light-blonde hair but whose teeth were large and white and free of any corrective metal.

"When I see the key," this girl said. "I think of a lock. Only there's no lock in the box."

Miss Meechum smiled.

"That's correct," she said. "And what about the seashell?"

The girl from Ohio thought about this for a moment, then replied, "Just like the key is alienated from its lock, the conch is removed from the ocean."

What followed was a conversation between Miss Meechum and this girl about how, due to the artist's arrangement, the items inside the box relied equally on what was present (e.g., the key, the shell, and the domino) as what was absent (e.g., the lock, the ocean, and the larger game). The torn music sheet that served as a background was, according to them, participating in this theme of alienation via its "missing notes."

Miss Meechum's point, as I understood it, was to think in terms of negation. Which is why, when I got home from school that day, I completely rearranged the contents of my capsule. No longer is the letter of introduction on top (nor, for that matter, does the letter contain all of its original pages). You still have my father's flathead screwdriver, but the two other tools have been returned to his workbench, along with certain pages of certain comics, the numerological interpretation of which, if properly sequenced, result in a coded message. Finally, the map of my neighborhood, which was once such a clean, coherent approximation, has been put through a wash cycle, left out in the sun, and burned in certain strategic locations.

It was hard to sleep that night. All I could do (from back here in the bombed-out past) was toss and turn, wishing I could live forever, or at least long enough to watch you make some sense of this assignment. I want to know what you find in the nothing. I want to know what you feel.

Negation, then, is a form of permission. It says, "You tell me what you need this to be."

Give me nothing, and I lean toward the fantastic. Such as the red-haired boy I saw in my neighborhood yesterday. He had set up a little card table where his lawn met the street, as if intending to sell lemonade. Except there was no lemonade. There was no product at all. He sat at the table, waving at all who passed and gesturing to a sign that read $5. Five dollars for what, though? A bracelet? A portrait? A riddle? To approach his table and ask would be to strangle the possibilities.

My mother was after my soul like the world itself was ending, but when it became clear I was not an easy convert, she enlisted the help of the youth pastor at the Methodist church. The youth pastor was a guy in his twenties who had two full sleeves of tattoos and slick black hair like something from *The Outsiders*. He played guitar in one of our town's only heavy metal bands, and he looked intense, but consensus said he was a Jesus freak, kind as they come. Per my mother's request, I sat down with him to talk about faith.

I told him about the night I threw rocks at the sky, and about the many nights I prayed for God to give me a sign of His existence.

"Keep throwing rocks," the youth minister said. "He'll throw something back."

I was listening, but I could not stop staring at the side of his neck, which cased a tattoo of a black snake pinned down by a switchblade. This death was not drawn in the crude, cartoonish style of the other tattoos I had seen. This was vivid. It was art. Every part of it—the blood-flecked scales, the play of light on blade's edge, even the tiny, agonized face of the snake—everything was rendered in the finest detail.

"And if He doesn't?" I said. "I'm told the world is ending, so I'd like to get my story straight."

At this, the youth pastor removed a small black-leather Bible from his pocket. He flipped to a page that contained many underlines and annotations.

"These are the words of Jesus," he said. "'I give them eternal life, and they will never perish, and no one will snatch them out of my hand.'"

He read this verse to me, stared hard into my face, then said, "Did you catch that? 'No one will snatch them out of my hand.'"

I stole a look at the snake, who was writhing beneath that blade.

"What does that mean?"

"It means that Christ loves you and that He already has you in His hand. Nothing—and I mean nothing—could compel Him to release you. Not death in December, not death a hundred years from now."

"But if He already holds me, what's left for me to do?"

"Believe."

He read me a few more verses then, on my way out, he gave me a flyer for his band. They were called The Sound of Our Hooves Carries News of Your Demise, and there was a picture of him in the middle of the flyer. He was jumping in the air with his guitar. I saw him, and I saw his snake. His eyes were closed, and his head was thrown back like a man possessed. Whatever sound he was after, he was not seeking it— he was believing in it.

The only faculty member who our parents liked less than Miss Meechum was Mr. Welsh, the Science teacher. When you asked your parents about Mr. Welsh, they would say, "He's a conspiracy nut." It was hard to contend with these designations.

"You are coming of age in the death rattle," Mr. Welsh told us on the first day of class. "In ten years, there will be a computer in everyone's house. In twenty years, there will be a computer in everyone's pocket. Enjoy reality while you can. It won't be with us much longer."

One day, Mr. Welsh opened our discussion with a VHS tape in which Noam Chomsky argued that, based on the Nuremberg Principles, every American president since Eisenhower was (legally speaking) a war criminal.

"These people do not want you free," Mr. Welsh said. "They want you numb, dumb, and distracted."

To Mr. Welsh's point, I had spent the past few years watching the kids in my neighborhood slowly disappear from the yards and the streets and the woods. Everyone was inside now. Everyone was in front of a screen.

"You want to come out?"

"Nah."

"It's beautiful out here. I was thinking of going down to fish in the creek behind Tripp's house."

"I can't. I'm in the middle of a show."

The down side: empty neighborhoods remind me of cemeteries. The bright side: you and I had autumn all to ourselves.

Miss Meechum told us to copy out our favorite quotation and put it in the time capsule, but I'm a quotation junkie, so I told her I would settle for a list of three. In went Thomas Wolfe, who said, "The whole conviction of my life now rests upon the belief that loneliness, far from being a rare and curious phenomenon, peculiar to myself and to a few other solitary men, is the central and inevitable fact of human existence." In went Howlin' Wolf, who said, "There ain't nothing but my troubles." In went Jesus, who said, "In this world, you will have trouble. But take heart! I have overcome the world."

I wrote another note. This time I kept it short: "*Sadie, I think everyone here is asleep—everyone except for you. That's one of the million reasons I want to be with you. I would like to be more awake.*" I wrote it, and Billy delivered it, and Sadie ignored it. The few times I worked up the courage to wave, she waved back, though always with a sneer, and never with any indication she had given my offer any further consideration.

"Doesn't protocol dictate that she respond?" I asked Billy, after a hard week of nothing. "If it's a no, it's a no, but she has to commit to the rejection, doesn't she?"

"Protocol?" Billy laughed. "Sadie's punk."

"Are punks against protocol?"

"No," Billy said. "They're above it."

Coming off Sadie's silence, I intended to pass October in obscurity. My mother had a different plan.

"You need to go somewhere," she said. "You need to get involved in something."

"Why?"

"Because people need people," she said. "It's one thing to be introverted, it's another to be isolated."

"What are you suggesting?"

"That's for you to figure out. I don't care what it is,

so long as it gets you away from that assignment and close to other humans."

I called my father, the mercenary, later that night.

"Don't think of it as socialization," he said. "Think of it as you've always thought of it—as material."

For the sake of material, and for the sake of staying busy, I tried to try something. There was a bulletin board at the front of the school with all extracurricular offerings. You read the little flyers to understand your options. There was wrestling and football in the fall, and baseball and track in the spring. There was Band if you played an instrument, choir if you could sing.

I saw a flyer for chess club, and thought I would start there. But the only information was a phone number, and when I called it, a man picked up and said, "Bunny? Bunny, is that you?"

I hung up and assumed that I misdialed. But when I dialed the number again, extra careful, extra slow, I heard the same man's voice on the other end.

"Bunny," he said. "Don't do this to me."

When I said nothing, he started to weep into the receiver and said, "I'm serious, baby, I don't think I'll make it without you."

I decided to try wrestling, which met everyday after school in a grimy room at the back of the gymnasium. In the room, there were filthy blue mats on the floor and a little rusted-out water fountain in the corner. Only half of the fluorescent lights worked, and of the tubes that worked, about half flickered, which made you feel like a hook-handed lunatic was about to jump out and kill you. There was the smell of bleach, and there was the smell of blood, and you never could be sure which one was stronger.

I showed up early to meet the coach, who I had heard was an old redneck named Gowers. There were five or six kids already practicing. Two of them, both lightweights, were down on the mat, stretching out. The rest were paired off and practicing moves. I looked around for Coach Gowers, but it was only us.

"Get loose," said a heavyweight with a fu manchu. "We start drills in five."

The facial hair, the deep voice, the stomach as big as a man's—here was a kid with authority. I joined the team on the filthy mat and began stretching. The other wrestlers were rough-looking, foul-mouthed, and violent, but all of them made a point to shake my hand and welcome me to the team.

"I'm Sticks," said a skinny kid with a shaved, scabby head.

"I'm Walpole," said another, extending a hand that was covered in warts that had been bitten down to bloody nubs.

"I'm Hambone," said the most normal looking kid in the room. "Real name Hamilton, but everyone calls me Hambone."

Exactly five minutes later, Fu Manchu clapped his meaty hands together and said, "Line up! Burpee time!"

Everyone, including me, obeyed, and for the next three hours, this is how it went—Fu Manchu would shout out an exercise, and the rest of us would comply.

"Give me ten bear crawls to the back of the mat and back! If I catch anyone slacking, I'll bust your fucking skull!"

"Our sprawls have looked like shit! I want one person shooting, and the other sprawling! Remember to stuff the head!"

"Head outside and give me two miles on the track! After that, we'll stretch and go home!"

Three hours passed in a blur, and when practice was over, I was soaked in sweat, bleeding from three different places on my face, and too weak to lift my arms.

After the rest of the team left, I talked to Fu Manchu, who was mopping the mats with a bucket of bleach.

"Where's Coach Gowers?" I asked.

"He had something come up," he said. "But I'll tell him you were here."

I went home, slept like a dead man, and came back the next day to find the exact same kids doing the exact same thing. Still no Coach Gowers.

"Get loose!" said Fu Manchu. "We start drills in five!"

I sat down on the mat beside Sticks, who was using a Gerber knife to scrape purple gum off the bottom of his shoe.

"Hey, Sticks," I said. "I have a question."

"What's that?" he said, still hard at work on the gum.

"Where is Coach Gowers?"

"I don't know," he said. "I guess he had something come up."

"Two days in a row?"

Sticks shrugged and, having worked the last of the purple gum off his shoe, he pocketed his knife and began his stretches. We stretched until Fu Manchu clapped his hands together and said, "Line up! Burpee time!"

For three hours, we stretched, we drilled, and we wrestled in that rank-smelling room with the slasher-movie lights. Wrestling was not kind to the body. A guy would get on top of you and run his grimy forearm across your face like a saw, trying to turn you over, or at least bloody you up. In response, you would reach back and tear at his face and his ears and his hair, all of it one sweaty, panting animal who you had to shake to stop the pain. The guy who had his hands on you was like a brother you were trying to kill, and you understood that he felt the same way about you. So you killed each other, and you kept killing each other, until Fu Manchu screamed, "Round!" at which point you stood up and shook hands.

When practice ended, Sticks and Walpole and Hambone said goodbye and stumbled home. Only Fu Manchu was left and, as before, he limped over to the mop and began cleaning the mats like a tired old man. I approached him, but before I could say anything, he spoke.

"I already know what you're going to ask," he said. "The answer is no. I don't know where Coach Gowers is, and I don't know when he's coming back. If that is a problem, then wrestling is not your sport."

Wrestling was my sport—for another week, at least. And in that week, Coach Gowers never did show up. New wrestlers joined the team (such as a pair of Mormon twins from Oklahoma), and old wrestlers left the team (such as Fu Manchu and a kid named Nut Nut). When Fu Manchu left, Sticks assumed a position of leadership. Sticks was there before you were, so as to shout (in a voice eerily similar to Fu

Manchu's), "Get loose! We start drills in five!" Sticks was there after you left, mopping those mats as if he had done so since eternity past.

I was leaving the gym one night, and I saw a new kid approach Sticks. He was a scabby 125-pounder who had recently moved down from West Virginia. He said, "Hey, Sticks, tell me the truth. There is no Coach Gowers, is there?"

Sticks did not hesitate in answering the question. "Coach is real," he said. "He had something come up, that's all. But I'll tell him you were here."

The West Virginian was clearly not satisfied by this.

"So what then?" he said. "Keep practicing? Keep waiting and hoping he'll show?"

Sticks smiled. "Now you've got it."

I watched the West Virginian limp out of the room, and I watched Sticks return to his lonely work of mopping the filthy mats. I knew, then, it was only a matter of time before Sticks disappeared and I was the one giving orders and answering questions. After that night, I never went back.

The next day at school, I checked the bulletin board to see if anything had changed. It had not. I tore down the flyer for Chess Club and, later that night, I tried the number again.

"Bunny?" said the man's voice. "Bunny, is that you?"

There was something in his voice, something frail but also indulgent. For no reason I could understand, I wanted to be cruel to this stranger.

"She's gone," I said. "Move on."

After this, a very sad and heavy silence. I thought about hanging up, but instead I stayed on the line and listened to him breathing. I knew what the breathing meant. It meant, "Who is this? Who the hell is this?" So I spared him the extra beat. I said, "Listen up—my name is Gowers, and I'm the new guy."

I kept trying to try. I tried football. First day out, during tackling drills, I hit the dummy in a way that was unacceptable to the supervising coach, who was a 400-pound lunatic from Mississippi who used to play center for the Falcons. Everyone called him "Sarge."

"Half-assed!" Sarge screamed. "Do it again!"

I hit the dummy again.

"Half-assed!" Sarge screamed. "Do it again!"

I wanted to walk away, but many movies in the back of my head said, "This is how growth happens. He's hard on you, then you're hard on yourself, and by the end of the season, the two of you will look back on this moment and laugh like father and son."

If Sarge had given me a few more seconds, I might have claimed this future for myself. The truth was, I had been feeling very cinematic lately. I had been thinking how good it would feel to get swept into something brutal and strange and beyond my control, something like football.

But when Sarge grabbed me by the facemask and grunted, "Cry for me, skidmark," I had no choice but to walk away. Material or no material, certain futures come to you thin as glass. These break on a single word.

I saw Miss Meechum sitting alone in the cafeteria. After getting my food, I joined her and asked what I had been wondering.

I said, "I heard they were going to fire you for the capsules."

She said, "I heard the same thing."

I said, "But if you know they are going to fire you, why don't you do something to prevent it?"

She said, "Because there's something worse than getting fired."

Back in The Pipe, this time with the weird ones of George MacDonald, when my mother looks in and starts up again with good intentions.

"What happened with wrestling?" she said.

"Wrestling is hard on the face," I said. "I don't have to be handsome, but I at least need to be palatable."

"Football?"

"Too concussive."

"What about Chess Club?"

"Too slow."

"You have to do something," she said. "You can't do nothing."

I wanted to say, "Or what?" What I actually said was, "Take it easy. I'll find something."

If you search for obscurity long enough, eventually, you'll find it. While riding my bike one afternoon, I saw a sign that read LIBRARY. I had not known that this side of town had a library, so I followed it. What I found, after cruising several blocks through a strange and oldish neighborhood, was a one-story house, red-brick and overrun by kudzu, set back on a dead-end road between a Baptist church and an abandoned roller skating rink. It was nothing like the county branch where my mother would take me on Saturdays. That library felt like a bank with its glass walls, and its large staff, and its thousands of glossy books. This library was the small opposite of all that. I left my bike outside and entered the building.

What hit you first was the smell, which was the warm hug of dust and ink and vanilla. Then you saw the wood floors and the cluttered shelves, the soft light and the un-dusted everything, and you felt alone, like you had stumbled onto a secret castle, and yet, at the same time, you felt watched, which was when you looked up saw that the person sitting behind the circulation desk was not a person—it was mannequin named Barry.

Barry is what the bronze name plate on the messy desk read. Barry was a middle-aged male who had been dressed in a brown tweed jacket, a pear-colored ascot, and oxford slacks, either in homage to or parody of the midcentury academic. He sat in the place of a librarian. A wine-red calabash pipe had been stuck into his mouth, and a paperback copy of Eliot's *The Waste Land* had been secured (via duct tape) to his right hand. Over his head hung a little plastic sign that read, HELP YOURSELF!

The first time I visited the library, I was certain someone was playing a trick. I checked the room (there was only one) to make sure that I was alone. I was. I checked the windows to make sure no one was outside. They weren't. I went back to the front (and only) door and saw that the locks had been removed.

I went next door to the Baptist church and talked to the preacher, who happened to be in his office.

The preacher was a large and perspiring man with a booming voice and the hair of Conway Twitty. His shirt was the color of mustard, and it had sweat stains under the arms and around the stomach. He worked a toothpick across his lips in a way that gave me the creeps, but he introduced himself as G.G. and talked to me like we were old friends.

"It's for real," G.G. said. "There's no locks on the door, so it's always open. Go on in and read your heart out."

"Okay," I said. "But who runs it?"

"No one," he said. "It runs itself."

"Aren't you, or they, or whoever, concerned that someone is going to break in and steal the books?"

G.G. laughed so hard at this that he had to remove the toothpick to keep from choking.

"Books?" he said. "Who would want to steal books?"

I thought about this for a moment and realized that, unless I wanted to risk sanctimony, there was nothing left to say. I got up to leave, but before I could, G.G. circled around and blocked the door. Between me and the world was the immovability of his mustard-colored gut.

"I can tell you're saved," he said. "It's the eyes that give it away."

I did not know how to respond to this, especially

since I had on my sunglasses, so I stood there and stared down at G.G.'s gatorskin shoes, which were also the color of mustard, and which seemed ready to explode under the pressure of his wide feet. G.G. lay a hand on my shoulder. Like a doctor in search of a tumor, he walked his big fingers across my clavicle and up to the little knob at the base of my skull, where he circled that bone with his heavy thumb and pressed down on it as if it were a button.

I did not have the courage to slap his hand away, but I did have the sense to step back and say, "What's your point?"

G.G. removed his toothpick and wagged it in perfect syncopation with his words.

"Don't get lost," he said. "Books are fine in doses, but stick with the Holy Ghost."

After I got out of G.G.'s office, I practically sprinted back to the library. It was as I had left it. The room was held in place by the smell of old books and the dusty bars of sunlight. Barry sat at his desk, the quietest kind of saint.

I went over to the shelves and began to look at the books. I looked until I found a title that I recognized—*Don Quixote*. I held the book in my hands. It was an old hardcover, heavy and yellowed and falling apart, but it felt good to have it in my hands. It felt better than a baseball, and it felt better than a

BB gun, and it felt better even than Sadie's hand. I carried it over to the library's one couch, which had been positioned under a window so as to catch all the best light, and I lay down in that light with the book in my hands, and because the quiet of that room was the kind that seems like an invitation for sound, I read the first sentence out loud. I said, "Somewhere in La Mancha, in a place whose name I do not care to remember, a gentleman lived not long ago..."

When I got home from the library, it was late.

"Where have you been?" my mother asked.

"I forgot to tell you," I said. "I decided to rejoin the wrestling team."

"Coach Gowers was okay with that?"

"Absolutely," I said. "He said the door is always open."

My character was shaped by my father, mainly his lines. Receive these from me, as I did from him.

Once, before the divorce, I dropped a ball that cost my team the championship game. It was night, and we were driving home, and as I leaned my head against the window and looked out at the darkness rushing past us, I was trying not to cry. Sensing this, my father punched me in the arm. This did what a good punch should do—it delivered me from that other, deeper pain.

"Listen," he said, "Some people love to win because a loss would crush them. Your job in life is to not be one of those people."

He preferred the aphorism, but sometimes he condensed his message into a single word.

When I complained about my school work: "Submit."

When a politician appeared on television: "Wolf."

Anytime "Maggie May" by Rod Stewart came on the radio: "Quiet."

His language was quirky but never careless. If he had no serious thoughts on a subject, he refused to pretend otherwise. "I got nothing," he would say, flashing his palms in apology. This was my favorite thing about him—that when he spoke, he gave you one or the other, either nothing or everything, but never some moderate banality, and never (thank God) pretense.

"Do you believe in love?" I asked him.

"I do," he said. "But only like I believe in ice cream."

"Any advice on confidence?" I asked him.

"Get a good haircut," he said. "The rest is faking it."

"Is the world really going to end? Are we going to die?"

"The world has always been going to end. And we've always been dying, just as we've always been living. Come January, expect the whole thing to continue stumbling forward. Us living but also dying. No one knowing and everyone pretending. Life, the whole tangled mess of it, each morning weird as the last."

You try to stay busy being obscure, but the world is busy being the opposite. I was at the library the other day, reading Tolkien and enjoying the light and the quiet, when the door opened and a face appeared. The face belonged to a boy about my age, only he had a vicious run of acne all over his face and neck, and he had a little sand-colored moustache that anyone could tell gave him great pleasure. He was smirking, and there was a lit cigarette fixed in the corner of his smirk. He looked like someone whose name was either Don or Ron, possibly Bret. He entered the library and walked straight up to me.

"You're kind of short," said the smoker.

I nodded my head, so as to imply, "Correct."

"Are you a midget?" he asked.

"No."

"You sure?"

"Yes."

He released an impressive plume directly into my face. I used the Tolkien to swat it away, a gesture I hoped might also convey my desire to swat him away. But the subtext was lost, and the smoker hung around.

"Did something stunt your growth?" he said.

"Possibly."

Cue the Southern sense of helpfulness: "You should eat more eggs. I hear eggs make you grow."

"Eggs," I said. "Got it."

"Does it bother you?"

"Not really."

"It would bother me."

It is probably a good thing I had a speech impediment. It meant silence (in the moment) and much composition (in the hours and days that followed).

My mother wanted me to surrender to Christ. I told her that I was done throwing rocks at the sky but that I remained open to a clue. Possibly in answer to her constant prayers, a clue did (eventually) appear. It came during a Sunday morning service that was so boring, I had no choice but to remove the Bible from the pew in front of me and begin reading.

I held the Bible by its spine and let the pages fall where they may. Split open before me was Chapter Fourteen of John's Gospel. To double down on the sense of destiny, I resisted the urge to begin reading at the top of the left page. I closed my eyes, brought the book to my face, and resolved to read whatever verse was directly in view.

And what I saw was this: "If anyone loves Me, he will keep My word; and My Father will love him, and We will come to him and make Our home with him."

If this verse was true, I had reversed the operation through which it became possible to encounter God. I had been searching for Christ Out There, throwing my rocks and demanding to see His face, when here in the plain words of the Nazarene, the exact opposite was laid out—Him making a home In Here. All this time I had been waiting for an invitation, when apparently He was waiting for the same thing.

I asked my mother that night, "Is it true that, if you ask Him, Christ will make His home inside your heart?"

"Yes," she said. "He comes in as the Holy Ghost."

"You've experienced this?"

"Yes."

"What does it feel like?"

My mother thought about this for a long time. Then she said, "Have you ever lost something, and it stays lost for a long time, but then you find it and feel very grateful?"

"Sure."

"That's what the Holy Ghost feels like. Familiar but also new. In John Chapter Three, Jesus compares Him to the wind."

"Why the wind?"

"Because you can't see Him, but you can feel Him. Because His movements are wholly beyond your control. And because there is nowhere on earth that He is not."

We sat there for a while, neither of us saying anything.

"I can pray with you," she eventually said. "I can ask the Holy Ghost to come into your heart. Would you like that?"

"Not right now," I said. "But maybe later."

I knew this was not the answer my mother wanted, but it was honest, and it was necessary. I was not ready to cast my lot with ghosts as big as the wind. I was barely cutting it as a seeker.

My mother was not the only evangelist in town. Take Miss Keegan, my Home Economics teacher. Having been tipped off by an anonymous source that I was "struggling with my faith," she invited me to eat lunch in her classroom. We sat on opposite sides of her desk. She sipped blackberry tea from a mug that read WASHED IN THE BLOOD. I pushed lukewarm Tater Tots across a Styrofoam tray and found places to look that were not her eyes.

She asked me for my thoughts on Christ, and I told her the truth.

"I love the Christ I read about in the Gospels," I said. "All that healing and teaching. All that love for the poor and the lowly. Wonderful stories, wonderful ideas."

"But?"

"But," I said, "this business about Him living inside of you—I don't know. I can read a story, and I can believe in a story, but I don't know how to let a story live inside me."

"You're asking some tough questions for a twelve-year-old," she said. "Is everything okay at home?"

"Home's good," I said. "No complaints."

"I notice that you keep referring to Christ as a story, not as a person. Is that because you can't see Him?"

"That's right."

"Let me ask you this," she said. "Do you feel that if you saw Him, even once, you could settle the issue?"

"Sure. If He's out there, and I see Him, I'll have no choice but to believe. But if He's not, I need to move on."

She sipped her tea and smiled a teacherly smile when I said this, all bright eyes and bunched cheeks.

"I admire your curiosity," she said. "Maybe you'll grow up to be a philosopher."

I thanked her for the compliment, despite the fact that I barely knew what a philosopher was. Then I asked her flat-out, "Miss Keegan, why did you want to have lunch with me?"

At this, she got up from her seat, checked the hallway for loiterers, and locked the door before returning to her desk. She pulled up a chair beside mine and scooted so close that I could smell the blackberry on her breath. She took my hands in hers and began to whisper, as if this new conversation had become something dangerous.

"Do you *really* want to see Christ?" she said.

"Yes."

"And you're willing to do whatever it takes?"

"Sure."

"Tell me this then—have you been baptized?"

I had been baptized twice—once by Baptists in a pond and again by Methodists in a pool. I reported both events to Miss Keegan, who was still bright eyed and smiling.

"Listen to me," she said and squeezed my hands so hard that it actually hurt the bones in my knuckles.

"I'm not talking about water baptism. I'm talking about true baptism. Baptism by fire."

I tried to free my hands, but Miss Keegan switched her grip, sliding down to my wrists and squeezing harder. I attempted to stand, but she yanked me back into my seat and drew closer to me, so close that we were almost kissing. Then she whispered, "Have you ever spoken in tongues?"

I don't know why I chose that moment to look directly into her eyes, but I did, and what I saw sobered me, wholly so, on the question of low churchgoers in the South. I saw—in their blueness, and in their brightness, and in their wild desperation to win me to her side—the eyes of a lunatic. If this was God's regional witness, I would content myself with apostasy.

"Miss Keegan," I said. "I need to ask you something."

She grinned and said, "I know what you're going to say because I'm gifted in discernment, but go ahead and say it anyway. Ask me for it."

I tore my hands away from hers and said, "May I go to the bathroom?"

Even the kids down here kept up their theologies.

"God is an old king with a long grey beard," said a kid with a pastor for a dad. "He sits on a throne made of light and has angels at His feet."

"So you've seen this?" I said.

"No," said the pastor's kid. "But the Bible's pretty vivid."

I got a different take from a brown-eyed girl with straight A's and the whitest pair of Keds in the world.

"It's pointless to *try* to see Christ," she said, bending down to brush a speck of dirt off her shoe.

"Why's that?"

"Because you've already seen Him. You're seeing Him right now."

This clean genius looked at me as if I should know what this meant. I didn't, and when I asked her for elaboration, she glared at me like I was a speck of dirt.

"Christ is not contained in any one thing," she said, still sneering. "He's in everything. Every sunset. Every blade of grass."

I appreciated the insight but could have done without the sneer. This girl was superior to me under every conceivable metric, and it seemed excessive to weaponize that discrepancy via the proud chin, the arched eyebrow, etcetera. She left me no choice but to say something dumb.

"Is Christ in those?" I said and nodded toward her shoes.

"Yes," she said and rolled her impossible brown eyes. "Christ is in those."

"What about these?" I said and submitted my own squalid, off-brand sneakers. "Is Christ even in these?"

She walked away and did not speak to me for the rest of the year. To her credit, I left that conversation with a new experiment. On the walk home, when I came across a caterpillar munching a hole through a maple leaf, I said, "Is that You, Lord?" Later that night, I sat on top of The Pipe and watched the sun go down. The sky caught fire with many brilliant shades of pink and blue and purple, and I looked at where the light was spilling over the tops of the trees, making that old orange empire into a new blue-gold one. I was alone and said to the trees, "That You?"

The Holy Ghost wanted space in my heart, but so did all the other stories. I attended the third best public middle school in Taylors, South Carolina, where stories buried themselves like mines in your brain and left you, after you'd heard them, waiting for the inevitable pop.

Some older boy at the lunch table would start it: "There's a perv in Del Norte who hands out tampered candy every Halloween. Razor blades in Reese's Cups. Anthrax in Pixy Sticks."

You had about seven seconds to contemplate this before someone else started in: "My cousin knows a guy who tapes infected needles to gas pump handles. By the time you realize what stuck you, it's too late."

Each new bomb would be more vile than the last, until someone said something that was too horrible to follow.

"My dad told me about this place he went to in college. It was called a glory hole. You could slip your dick through a hole in the wall and, on the other side, there'd be a whore who would suck you off. Except this one night, instead of a whore on the other side, there was a psychopath with a pair of garden shears."

You left these conversations and returned to a classroom where Coach Mac would read aloud a passage from Jack London, expecting it to thrill you. The sentences were nice, and you saw where someone might come away with a new perspective, but after the bombs of the cafeteria, literature hit with the force of a nursery rhyme. You sensed on such days that you had arrived at a place beyond the reach of language, possibly beyond the reach of love and of Christ, a place where only more filth (and possibly good music) could remind you how it felt to be alive.

"Draw close to Him," said my mother, the other night, after prayers. "And He will draw close to you."

"Closeness freaks me out."

"Give me your hand," she said. "I want to pray for you."

I gave her my hand and half-listened to her sweet words. But while she prayed, my mind was circling back to the gloryhole and the garden shears.

"As soon as you make space in your heart," she said. "He will enter."

"That's fine," I told her. "But my heart's a bit cluttered right now."

Whenever I began to feel sorry for myself for being a short kid with a speech impediment who split his love between the untouchable past and an unmovable punk, I considered the new kids and felt immediately grateful for my station in life. The newest of all was Christopher O'Sullivan, who had moved down from Boston. Christopher had copper-colored hair and was tormented because of his accent, and because of his not having a girlfriend, and (most of all) because of his failure to have been born in the same place as us. His real name was Christopher, but everyone called him Chrissie.

At recess, Rusty Riggins would put Chrissie a sleeper hold and say, "Here comes the dockness" until Chrissie passed out. One time Chrissie stayed unconscious for so long that Rusty retrieved a cup of water from the spigot then poured the water on the crotch of Chrissie's jeans and said, "Damn Yankee pissed himself!"

In return for this pain, Chrissie hit back at nobodies such as me. He hit back with facts.

"You know where South Carolina ranks in education?" he said.

"No."

"Forty-eighth," he said. "You know what that means?"

"No."

"It means that except for West Virginia and Mississippi, it doesn't get any dumber than here."

"Okay."

"It also means that it's not wise to screw your cousin."

Another time, at lunch, Chrissie sucked his teeth at my pair of peanut-butter and marshmallow sandwiches. I had the two sandwiches, a bag of chips, and a juicebox.

"Don't eye my food," I said. "Eye your own food."

"It's no wonder you people are so far behind. Look at the shit you eat."

I took a bite of my sandwich and washed it down with a squirt from my juicebox. I told him I couldn't see the connection between bad thinking and bad food. He said it wasn't worth the time it would take to spell it out.

"That math we're doing in class," he said. "I already did it back in Boston. In third grade. That's how messed up this place is. You've got sixth graders who can barely do third grade math."

"That's great," I said. "Easy A for you."

"Here's one," he said. "Do you know where this shithole ranks in terms of poverty?"

"No."

"Forty-second," he said. "Do you know what that means?"

"No."

"It could mean that you're dumb because your poor. But more likely it means that you're poor because you're dumb."

"Okay."

"You remember the other day when someone asked Miss Meechum what 'magnanimous' means?"

I told him I did remember this and that, in fact, I remembered the definition of 'magnanimous.' Magnanimous, according to Miss Meechum, meant 'having to do with lava, volcanoes, and that kind of stuff.'

"That's nowhere close to what that word means," he said. "Even the teachers down here are intellectually impoverished."

Chrissie kept talking, but I gathered my food and moved to a new table. I didn't leave because his argument was offensive. I left because it lacked insight. I already knew that Southerners abused the English language. I already knew that the food we put into our bodies was poison. And thanks to the never ending stream of kids from Boston and Ohio and Michigan (not to mention New York, New Jersey, and Philadelphia) I had long been aware that if there was a form of success that could be measured on a metric, South Carolina would come out near the bottom.

The last time I saw Chrissie, he was sitting by himself beneath the maple tree at the far edge of the playground. He was reading a book, which is what I planned to do with my recess. I thought about going over to him and asking if I could sit down beside him and read my book. If nothing else, I wanted to tell him that I had taken the time to look up the word 'magnanimous' in the dictionary.

I found a different tree, on the opposite side of the playground, and I didn't look in Chrissie's direction. If I started to think about him, I stopped. I had my own assignment to worry about. I had not much time left on the wonderful dying earth and many more words to learn.

"The people down here," said my cousin from Indiana, who was visiting for the week. "They're like cars with no brakes."

I considered asking him what he meant by this but decided against it. There's more mileage in ambiguity.

I did not resent my mother constantly sharing her theology with me. With school being fifty percent depravity and fifty percent banality, I appreciated any theology I could come by.

I loved the theology of Saint Paul, who says in his letter to the Corinthians, "If Christ has not been raised, your faith is futile." The question on Paul's mind seems to be, "What if God is a ghost we invented to feel better about ourselves?" His response: "Then we of all people are most to be pitied."

I loved the counter-theology of Bill Hicks, who said, "I'm tired of this back-slappin' isn't-humanity-neat bullshit. We're a virus with shoes."

I loved theology, but I doubted theologians. I tried to trust everyone, but in the end, I never trusted anyone. Not Paul the Apostle, not Bill Hicks, not even my own mother. None of them began their message with the one thing I needed to hear: "I have no idea what is happening here. We have neat theories, and we have deep fears, but at the end of the day, we're all waiting around to see what might happen." Confidence is easy. Give me unknowing. Give me wonder.

More and more we heard rumors that Miss Meechum was being let go at the end of the year. She addressed them in class with characteristic ferocity.

"The house is on fire," she said. "And your parents want to paint the porch."

Rusty Riggins found Billy Beale alone at recess. Pretending he was a medieval knight, Rusty chased Billy into the woods, then used a sock full of pennies to install bruises on his face, arms, and stomach. Before leaving, Rusty screamed, "Excelsior!"

Miss Meechum was already in trouble for the capsules. She made it slightly worse with a homework assignment that read: "In no less than 500 words, please argue which historical figure you would assassinate, if armed with a time machine, unlimited weapons, and legal immunity." I say "slightly," because everyone in the class wrote the same essay about how they would prevent the Holocaust by eliminating Hitler. The only parent who complained was the mother of the student who wrote about killing Thomas Jefferson.

"I don't see the educational merit in this," this mother was alleged to have said to Miss Meechum. "I don't get it."

Her response: "You're not supposed to."

What a machine the heart can be. I feared and hated Rusty Riggins from the moment I met him, and now that we were in middle school, and Rusty was still the supreme agent of pointless violence, I loathed him even more. He still choked kids out, and he still bit the inside of his cheek and stared at you like a psycho as the blood dribbled down his chin. And yet, what of the day at the bus stop when Rusty picked a fight with an eighth grade transplant from Ohio and got knocked out cold? I watched with the crowd as this large stranger snapped Rusty with a vicious right cross. I watched Rusty fall and crack his head on the pavement. I should have thought, "What goes around, comes around." Instead, I thought, "Get up, Rusty! Get up!"

I was never cruel to my mother, but occasionally I was rude. Such as the lovely Saturday morning she attempted to confiscate my capsule and drive me out of The Pipe to play with other kids. Except that I didn't want to leave The Pipe, and I had nothing to say to other kids. And so I told her, "You have your garage, I have my box. You're storing up canned goods because you think the world's ending, I'm storing up memories because I'd like it to continue. Are we all that different?" She walked away from this one, and returned to the garage, where she had been assembling mini first aid kits, and I moved to my room and continued work on the capsule. Since my room was directly above the garage, I could hear her down there working. I never felt so close to her as on those long, quiet Saturdays where we were alone and engrossed, each of us holding oblivion at bay through a series of careful adjustments.

I snuck out of bed one night and went down to the garage, where I spied on my mother. She was on her knees, testing the batteries of various flashlights and radios. Her face as she performed this work could not have been more serious. Her lips moved, and though I couldn't hear her words, I knew that she was praying.

On the phone with my father, I said, "You asked me the other night what I would want if the world really was going to end. Here it is—I want you to come back home, and I want you and Mom to start over."

Him: I wouldn't hold your breath for that. We have a complicated history.

Me: Then rearrange it. Make it simpler.

Him: Like your shoebox?

Me: Exactly.

Him: Maybe lived life is a bit more tricky.

Me: Maybe you lack imagination.

I have included here a picture of Elvis. Not the young, slim Elvis of the fifties, but the other one. The fat one, and the puffy-haired one, and the one in white sparkly jumpsuits. I trust that you will know that this picture signifies the time I snuck out of bed and found my parents watching an Elvis concert on television. It was late and we had school tomorrow, but there was Elvis sitting at a piano. He was so large and sweaty, so happy and sad at the same time. I asked to stay up and watch.

"One song," said my mother.

The one song was "Unchained Melody."

My dad said, "Listen closely. This might be the best love song ever written."

I listened and this is what Elvis sang: "Time goes by so slowly. And time can do so much. Are you still mine?"

He paused and smiled at the camera. "I need your love," he sang in a lower, more desperate voice. "I need your love."

I fell asleep that night thinking about how, when Elvis sang about love, it seemed like something I could believe in. I liked that he told the truth about time. I liked that he sang about needing but never getting.

The next day, I told my father, "When Elvis comes to Greenville, let's you and me go see him."

I pretended not to be sad as he told me that Elvis was dead. I pretended not to be horrified as he told me how it happened.

My neighbor, the same boy who showed me the bat, found me in The Pipe and told me about a murder.

"This is a true story," he said. "It happened in those apartments down there."

"What happened?"

"Two men broke into a woman's home. They beat her up and stole her money. Then they killed her. They might've done more."

"They get caught?"

"One man did. He's in jail right now. They say he'll get the chair."

"And the other?"

"They never found him," my neighbor said. "Some say he's dead. Most think he's still out there."

Rusty Riggins was still out there. And yet, his stories were in here, and those said he was choking everything in sight. Something in my heart knew it: before the world ended, I would have to fight him. I began to prepare for the inevitable.

"Christ says to turn the other cheek," my mother said. "Some have tried to make this metaphorical, but I don't think it is."

That was about as encouraging as a migraine. So I asked my father.

"Fighting rednecks is like dumping money on a carnival game," he said. "Even if you win, what's the prize?"

This felt true but lacking in practicality, so I turned to Billy Beale. Billy answered the question with no hesitation.

"Kick him in the dick," he said. "Forget all those dumb rules about what makes a fight clean. They're bullshit. When Rusty tries to grab you, kick him as hard as you can directly in his crotch. The purists will call this dirty, but they've never been in a fight, or else they'd know that all violence is dirty."

Further research was pursued via cartoons, most of which featured the classic bully-versus-shy-guy plot. Their moral was Darwinian in nature: "Bullies prey on the weak. Stand up for yourself, and they'll leave you alone." Their episodes depicted a victim who, having stood up to his oppressor, puts an end to the cycle of violence and wins the respect of his peers.

I had a plan: when Rusty bullied me, I would not kick him in the dick, and I would not turn the other cheek, but I would brandish enough confidence to send him off in search of more vulnerable prey. I would be confident. I could be confident. As long as I had my sunglasses, I could look confident.

Mr. Welsh: They say Elvis is dead. I don't believe
   them.
  Me: Where is he?
  Mr. Welsh: Where else? Out there.

There were nights when I felt sure the Holy Ghost was real and the only thing keeping me from asking Him into my heart was my inability to surrender my fetish for evidence. But then there were nights when my heart seemed too sad a machine to have come from a King the likes of Him. The problem was, I could see it both ways. Like many Southerners, I felt ruined by possibilities.

Back here, the kids were cruel, but the teachers were kind. Teachers were rendered useless by their kindness, which was bottomless and indiscriminate. We might have ranked forty-eighth in education, but we felt invincible when these paunchy, blue-eyed white women floated around the room reminding us how intelligent and how talented and how wonderful we all were. Their sense of mercy was something out of the Bible. Rusty Riggins could break a kid's nose, and the world would call him a monster, but not his teacher. His teacher would kneel beside him and say in the voice of an angel, "Let's think about this for a moment, Rusty. How would you feel if someone broke your nose?" Teachers only wanted to develop you into a somewhat decent human being. In return, you skulked around their sad little rooms, half-grateful and half-ashamed, because all you wanted was lunch, recess, and to be left the hell alone to think the thoughts that actually mattered.

Did kindness survive the apocalypse? It baffled me, back here, to witness even small acts of kindness. Kindness here was like a car crash or a house fire. If you ever bore witness to it, you told the story for years to come and assumed no one believed it.

"Kindness requires calculation. And Americans don't want to slow down long enough to do math. We hurtle forward, such cannonballs since forever."
—Coach Mac

"Kindness is fear in a dress. Give me the other, uglier way. Give me reality." —My father

My mother had her own kindness. Nightly, she asked if I wanted to invite Christ into my heart. I was being truthful when I told her that, although I could not invite Christ into the capsule of my heart, at the same time, I could not get Him out of my head. I thought about Him at school, I thought about Him at home, and I especially thought about Him while laying in bed at night. What I thought about, primarily, were the stories where He revealed Himself to onlookers, not in a dream, and not in a vision, but in reality. Moses and the burning bush. The cloud on Mount Sinai. Thomas with his fingers in the holes of the risen Lord. I craved such palpability. I needed Christ the Person, not Christ the Myth. I needed the Holy Ghost to be a little less like the wind and a little more like a pair of sunglasses.

Having heard all this, my mother said, "You have to believe."

What I said next was the closest thing to honesty I ever shared with my mother.

"I want to be saved and live forever," I said. "But I also don't want to lie."

He found me like he found everyone. It was at recess on a lovely fall day. I was drawing in the dirt with a stick when a particularly fat shadow fell over me. I looked up and it was Rusty, smiling the smile of a man who gives out damage without fear of taking on damage.

I stood up and, securing my sunglasses, I said, "Listen, Rusty, I had a long night and a rough morning. I'm in no mood to be messed with. If you know what's good for you, you'll keep moving."

I delivered this line flawlessly, never breaking eye contact. Rusty's eyes flicked back and forth from my face to my fists and, after a few tense moments, he muttered, "Fair enough," and backed away.

I knelt in the dirt and resumed my drawing, which was of a young elf drawing water from a brook. I was applying some lines to his tunic when Rusty's arm wrapped itself around my neck. He lifted me off the ground as I clawed at his meaty forearms and struggled to breathe.

The last thing I did before losing consciousness was try to swing my leg backward and kick Rusty in the dick. I can't speak toward the success of this attempt, since the next thing I remember is waking up in the dirt. My pockets were empty, my sunglasses were smashed to pieces, and in the branches overhead, my shoe was swinging like a pendulum.

If one good thing came from this incident it was that Rusty Riggins was no longer a myth. He had appeared to me. He had made his presence felt.

My father: I heard you got your ass kicked.

Me: It's true.

My father: Good. You wouldn't want the world to end without having checked that off the list.

Me: I forgot. Your generation thinks fighting makes you tough.

My father: Not tough. Just humble.

Here is a question that arose during morning devotionals.

"Hey, Mom," I said. "When Christ is on the cross, why does He say that God has forsaken Him?"

"Because that is how He felt," my mother said. "Because that is how it feels to be human—lonely and left out, forgotten by the one who loves you most."

With definitions such as this, I was closer than ever to becoming a true believer.

I was thinking about the importance of relationships, so I bought a goldfish and named him Tiger. I invited Billy Beale over to witness this, and he came, and we filled a small glass bowl with water and covered its bottom with neon-blue pebbles. We installed a pink plastic castle, very magisterial, in the event that Tiger required a break. This all took place on the kitchen table and, for the better half of an hour, Billy and I watched Tiger like a pair of rapt moviegoers.

"Look!" someone would say. "He's going into the castle!"

Several minutes later: "Look! He's coming out of the castle!"

Like certain stories I have since removed from this capsule, this was a thrill until it wasn't.

The youth pastor with great greased-up hair and the snake tattoo was fired from the Methodist church. No one was clear on the reason why. One theory was that he got caught drinking in the church basement. Another had it that he used the word "pussies" (in reference to the Pharisees) during one of his Wednesday night sermons.

He disappeared from our church instantly, and I assumed that it would be a long time before I saw him again. I was wrong about that.

Early one Saturday morning, about a week after he got fired, there was a knock on the front door of our house. Since I was the only one awake, I approached the peephole and looked out. It was him.

He had shaved off all of his great hair, and, although only a week had passed, he seemed much fatter than before, sweating heavily in a dress shirt and khakis. Between his outfit and the little rolling suitcase at his side, I gathered he was selling something. He stood there on my porch and smiled—not his old youth pastor's smile, but his new solicitor's smile.

He knocked several more times and never stopped smiling, but I never opened the door. I watched him through the peephole. He had pulled his shirt collar as high as it could go, but I knew exactly where to look. There was the knife, and there was the snake.

When my mother said, "Who was at the door?" I replied, "Just a salesman."

By the end of October, my capsule was cluttered with existence. The air was getting colder. The leaves outside the window were wine-red and fewer by the day. The talk about the end of the world was ongoing and increasingly serious. My mother continued stockpiling. My father told me everything was going to be okay. I did not know what else to do, so I kept adding to the assignment. I kept looking.

Billy Beale drew close to Jesus. He called a couple days before Halloween and told me so. He told me how it happened (tent revival, altar call), then he told me that the Holy Ghost, who now dwelled inside his heart, had compelled him to confess something.

"Remember those notes you asked me to give to Sadie?" he said.

"Yes."

"I never delivered them."

"What?"

"Yeah, I never actually gave those to Sadie."

"What did you do with them?

"I threw them away."

"But you told me that you gave them to her."

"I lied."

"Why would you do that?"

There was a long pause, after which Billy said, "I don't know. This was back before I met the Lord, so who can say what was happening in my heart. But now that I'm a Christian, I feel horrible for having lied to you. I hope you'll forgive me."

"Wait," I said. "So Sadie doesn't know?"

"Nope," he said. "But look on the bright side, you still have time to tell her."

I wrote one last note. I lacked the heart for anything except the question itself. The next day, at recess, I walked up to Sadie, who was sitting by herself and listening to overly loud punk on her big red head-phones, and I placed the note directly into her hand. She stared at the note, then she stared at me. The look on her face said, "This must be a mistake."

After recess, Sadie disappeared. She never came back to class, and once the day was over, she never showed up to the bus stop. I looked all over school, and I asked the few kids who were still around, but eventually it became clear she was gone.

I ran back to Miss Meechum's room, which looked sad now that no one was in it. Miss Meechum was sitting at her desk and staring at the empty room. Her eyes looked different, as if she had been crying. There were rumors (or we had heard there were rumors) she was going to be fired after Christmas break on account of the assignment.

"Miss Meechum," I said. "What happened to Sadie?"

"I'm sorry," she said. "But Sadie went home early. She wasn't feeling very well."

I did not know what this meant, but I thanked Miss Meechum anyway, and I walked home. The air outside was cold and smelled of candy. Skeletons dotted lawns. Sad flags danced on all the porches.

Here is a photograph from Halloween night. Look at me: fat Elvis. Look at Billy Beale: either a pirate or a gypsy (can you tell which?). We were ready to go trick-or-treating, but it was not yet dark enough. And so we hung back in the kitchen with our flashlights and pillow cases, and we watched Tiger swimming circles around his bowl.

"I saw this circus performer once," said Billy. "He swallowed things."

"What kind of things?"

"For starters, a sword."

Billy paused and indicated with his hands the impressive length of the blade. I did the math and it seemed barely but technically possible.

"How did that not kill him?" I said.

"It should've. But he knew the secret."

The secret—there was one in every story. But you never stopped to ask what it was because to do that would've marked you as curious, and curious was the opposite of cool, since the coolest people you knew seemed to have all the answers and, on top of that, were impressed by nothing. I stared at Tiger in his bowl and nodded my head as if to say, "Ah, so he knew the secret. Good for him."

"After the sword," he continued. "He swallowed a woman's wedding ring. This married woman was appalled for about seven seconds. Then he straightened a metal hanger, ran it straight down to his stomach, and fished it out."

I thought about the metal hangers in my closet, which made my throat itch. I secretly scratched off 'performative swallower' from my list of potential careers.

"But his last and best trick was when he swallowed a goldfish."

"How'd he get a fish back up?" I said. "The hanger?"

"Nope. He took the fish bowl like this and—"

Here Billy stopped and began to convulse, as one does when preparing to vomit.

"Bleh!" he said, jutting out his chin and unfurling his tongue. "Like that, the fish was back in the bowl."

I attempted to imagine this, which required envisioning the poster that hung in Mr. Welsh's Science Corner. The poster featured a cartoonish diagram of the mouth connecting to the throat, the throat joining up with the esophagus, and the esophagus descending like a rabbit hole into the wide brown cave of the human stomach. I imagined Tiger travelling down such apparatus, then I imagined him making the same journey in reverse. My conclusion: "Why not?"

It was decided: someone would swallow Tiger.

We flipped coins, and I lost, so I reached into the bowl, plucked out Tiger on the first try, and flung him down my throat like a slick, oversized pill. I opened my mouth, and I stuck out my tongue. Billy nodded in approval.

"How does it feel?" he asked, nodding toward my stomach.

I wanted to say something clever but couldn't think of anything good. So I said, "It feels like there's a fish swimming around in my stomach."

Billy laughed and said, "Let's get him out."

He grabbed the fish bowl and held it under my face. I stuck two fingers down the back of my throat. I heaved and spewed out some water. I heaved again and more water spilled out. I was about to try a third time and felt confident that, on this attempt, Tiger would take flight from my mouth and spin through the air like some winged creature from a fairytale. But just as I slid my fingers into my mouth, there was a knock at our front door.

I ran down the hall and answered it. I opened the door, figuring it would be one of the kids from the neighborhood. It wasn't. Waiting on my front porch was Sadie Hayes. She was dressed like Rosie the Riveter, and she was holding my note.

"Hey," she said and smiled at me.

"Hey," I said and smiled back.

She extended her hand into the space between us. She said, "Let's go."

I looked at my block, which had gone dark except for the streetlamps. Tiger was on the move inside of me, and I could hear Billy's voice back in the house. I believe he was calling my name. Except none of that was real anymore. I took off my sunglasses, at which point Sadie took off her headphones. I put my hand in hers, and together we walked into the night.

November 1999

Miss meechum was right when she said writing is the only thing in the world that makes you feel like you are kicking Death in his teeth. What she neglected to mention is that being in love is the only thing in the world that kicks writing in its teeth. Forgive the dearth of material for the month of November. Sadie had me.

I didn't know what dating entailed and, as such, during all my firsts—my first date, my first kiss, my first fight—I kept expecting some jerk with a whistle to appear out of nowhere and expose me as a fraud. After several blistering and sanctimonious toots, this skidmark would take Sadie by the hand and announce, "You'll have to come with me. This one has no clue what he's doing." This fear often symptomized as a prickle in my scalp, and though it faded over time, it never completely went away. I figured things out in time, but I was always waiting for someone with more credentials to tell me I was finished.

Sadie and I spent most of our time at The Pipe. Sadie would bring her guitar. I would bring my capsule. We did our work in that subterranean silence until it got dark outside, at which point we would climb out, and I would walk her home.

Sadie always did the same thing when we stood outside of her mother's trailer. She would grab me by the shirt and pull me into her. We would hold each other in the cold, and she would kiss me hard on the lips and say, "Don't die." I would kiss her back and say, "I'll do my best."

This seems morbid, until you realize that nearly everything with Sadie came down to death.

On school: "A system that cultivates intellectual death."

On America: "A country founded on death, dependent on death, and now inseparable from death."

On the Millennium: "The big death. The death of all deaths. Thank God, it's about time, bring it on baby, the capital-D Death."

No kind of evangelist, Sadie did, on several occasions, attempt to woo me into this necrotic tilt.

"This world hates you," she said to me, one day in The Pipe. "It hates the way you look. It hates the way you talk. And for the last twelve years, it has seized every opportunity to remind you that you don't belong here. You're dead to it, and yet, you won't concede that it's dead to you? Wake up, man."

I thought, in that moment and in many moments that followed it, about giving to Sadie everything I had given to you. I considered giving her the capsule and saying, "If you look through this and still believe that the earth is a dead place, then you know little about the world and nothing about me." I thought all of this in the strong, clear voice of my head; but when it was time to speak such things with the dumb, clumsy voice of my mouth, I said, "I don't know, Sadie. It's not so bad here, is it?"

She called me a fool before pushing me down onto

the cold floor of The Pipe and biting my lip like a beautiful lunatic. For someone who worshiped the ubiquity of death, she was the most alive person I knew.

You should know that, across the month of November, there were many tender moments involving Sadie. Kind words, selfless gestures, even a bit of vulnerability. But when she looked inside my capsule and found a record of these decencies, she demanded I omit them. When I asked why, she said, "Because some stranger in the future doesn't get to see that side of me. You earned it. He didn't."

When it wasn't about death with Sadie, it was about punk. More specifically, it was about what was and what wasn't punk. I let this go for a while, but one day in The Pipe, my curiosity eclipsed my need to seem cool, and I asked her straight out: "What is punk?"

I expected her to know the answer straight off, and she did.

"Punk is not a movement," she said. "It's a condition of the soul."

"But what does it stand for?"

"Nothing," she said. "It stands against. You find

out what you're supposed to do, then you do the opposite."

"Who is punk?"

"Joe Strummer."

"Who is the opposite of punk?"

"Everyone down here."

"Even me?" I said.

"Especially you."

"Then why are you with me?"

"Because I'm not supposed to be," she said. "Why are you with me?"

"Because I like you."

"See," she said. "That's not punk."

You will have guessed by now that my mother was not a fan of Sadie. Originality was fine in the abstract, but there's something about a mohawk that breaks a mother's heart.

"I saw Casey Hubbard at the grocery," she told me. "She sure is cute."

"I'm bit," I said.

"That blonde hair. Those freckles. You know she asked about—"

"Freckles are not punk."

Sadie was not a conversationalist. I pursued her through lists.

Me: Top three candies.

Sadie: Warheads, Cry Babies, Sour Patch Kids.

Me: Top three movies.

Sadie: *Blue Velvet, Pulp Fiction, Texas Chainsaw Massacre.*

Me: Top three fears.

Sadie: I don't have three fears. I barely have one.

Me: What is it?

Sadie: Predictability.

I am obsessed with lists, and for this we thank my father, who was incapable of answering an open-ended question with a single, declarative statement.

The answer to, "Who's your favorite band?" was never as simple as "The Stones." It was always the long pause while he considered your question from various angles. After the pause, he would request qualification: "What genre?" Having received this, he only needed only several seconds to form a three-item list (always in ascending order and always delivered as if the rankings were inevitable): "Okay, well if we're talking about singer songwriters, my number three is Prine, my number two is Dylan, and I'm going to have to give number one to Waits."

The people back here loved stories, but I preferred the list. After someone tells me a story, I cannot shake the feeling that they have been split into clones: the version of the self that appears in the story, and the version of the self that narrates that appearance. I never know which version is true, and I get even more dizzy when someone repeats the same story in a slightly different construction, thereby making clones of the clones and leaving me baffled as to who the hell is talking. Stories obscure (even as they shine). Lists do the opposite. They reveal. They say, "I cut everything that wasn't me. Here is what survived." A good list is an arrangement of desire.

Sadie was from Florida, but she didn't like to talk about it. She once called Florida "a wound dressed up like a party." She once said, "Florida is the place where emergencies go to die."

"You think you know something about it," she told me. "Because you think Florida is in the South. But Florida does not belong to the South."

"What does Florida belong to?" I asked.

"Itself."

November was school work and home work and, once those banalities fizzled, the long afternoons at The Pipe and the longer nights at the firepit outside of Sadie's trailer, all of it golden, and all of it seeming, with Y2K right there, to be thrumming with the stupidly good goodness of life.

"Stay," she would say to me, those days at The Pipe, when neither of us had eaten anything for hours, and I would attempt to sneak out for food.

"I'm hungry," I would say. "Aren't you hungry?"

"I am," she would say. "But let's stay for a little bit longer."

It was the same for those nights at the fire pit outside her trailer, especially when we were drinking cold cans of cheap beer.

"Stay," she would say to me, when the fire was all but dead, and my curfew was long since busted.

"I have to go home," I would say. "I'm going to be in trouble."

"I know," she would say. "But stay anyway. We'll be dead in December. There's only so much trouble you can get into when you're this close to the end."

Last night I stayed out until 3 a.m. before returning home slightly drunk but deeply happy. Not even the tears on my mother's face could diminish my sense of resignation.

Not everything at school was banal. Sometimes strangeness found you.

"Do you believe in ghosts?" a shy girl with a large forehead and gold-frame glasses asked me the other day.

I told her I didn't, and she said, "You will after this."

For the next ten minutes, I stood there and listened to this kindly classmate say one disturbing thing after another.

She told me about a hillbilly killer with a hook for a hand who stalked the cars on lover's lane.

She told me about a girl who got bit on the cheek by a spider and how the bite got bigger and bigger, until one day (as the girl was attempting to make out with her boyfriend) the swollen wound exploded and hundreds of baby spiders spilled out onto the boyfriend's face.

She told me about a woman named Alice who was murdered by her husband and buried in a hilltop cemetery less than a mile from our school. The husband killed Alice because he had fallen in love with their maid, who was (according to the girl with glasses) "a bony little thing with a hamster for a brain." Immediately following the murder, the husband slipped the wedding ring off Alice's finger and proposed to the maid, who was so enthused by this twist of fate that she put on the ring and danced circles around Alice's corpse.

"Alice's body was buried, but her soul can't move on until she finds her ring."

"That's horrible," I said.

"That's nothing," she said. "I heard if you visit her grave at midnight, and if you hold your hand directly over her tombstone, the rings on your fingers will spin. That's the ghost of Alice searching for her wedding band."

The girl smiled as she said this. I could see her blue eyes shining behind the glasses with a weird kind of ecstasy. I wanted to ask her why all the girls at our school loved horror stories, but before I could, she said, "One more."

I agreed and next she told me about Bloody Mary and how, if I stood in front of a mirror, turned off the light, and called her name thirteen times, when I turned the lights back on, Mary would appear.

"Mary looks different each time," she said. "The first time I saw her, she was covered in blood and screaming at me. She was reaching for my neck and threatening to strangle me. The second time I saw her, though, she was in a sundress, and she was perfectly happy. She smiled and told me, 'Don't believe a word they say about love.'"

I had heard this story on several different occasions and in several different forms. In fact, I had performed the experiment at least three times, in strict compliance with the rules that were supposed to invite Mary into the mirror. But no matter how many times I called Mary's name, she never showed up. This report troubled the girl with glasses.

"And you said her name exactly thirteen times?"

"Yeah."

"And it was completely dark?"

"Yeah."

"And you kept the fingers of your left hand crossed the entire time?"

I admitted I had never heard the bit about the fingers. This made the girl smile. The last thing she said to me before walking away was this: "If you want to see her, follow the rules." That sounded too close to the things I heard in church. I forgot it immediately and returned to my capsule.

Me: Top three Biblical figures.

My mother: Counting Christ?

Me: No, that's cheating.

My mother: Let's see, then. Number three, David. Number two, Ruth. Number one, Job.

Me: Why's Job number one?

My mother: Because any jerk can worship God in
the midst of prosperity. Job worshipped
in the midst of suffering. Try losing everything and loving the one who took it.

Lists require commitment. I get tired of genres
obsessed with their own capacity for accomodation.
Give me a good list, which says, "I have room for
three, and I'm leaving now. Who's in?"

One night at her trailer, Sadie proposed a trade. It
was cold for a fall night in Carolina, and we had a
good fire going. We were holding each other and
secretly working on some blackberry wine that her
mother had left out.

"Leave your capsule with me," she said. "And take
mine home with you."

"Why?"

"Why else?" she said, smiling. "So we can understand each other."

I thought about this. I did not, in principle, disagree.

"Okay," I said. "But look. I've worked hard on that
arrangement."

"What do you take me for?" she said. "A thief?"

"Yes," I said and reminded her that yesterday in Wilson's Five and Dime she had stolen two bags of Skittles, a pack of mini lighters, and a keychain that said WORLD'S COOLEST UNCLE.

"No stealing," she said. "Just looking."

Before leaving her trailer that night, Sadie gave me her capsule, which was painted black and, based on its weight, all but empty. I gave her mine, which contained every memory worth preserving. I knew that she would take something, and I knew that when I asked, she would lie about it. I didn't care. I wanted it to happen this way. I wanted a love that consisted precisely of this—your favorite person in the world, sitting alone in a room across town, deciding what to steal from all your favorite memories.

I waited until I got home to open Sadie's capsule. I waited until I was in my bedroom, and the door was locked, and everything was dark, and it was just me on the floor with a flashlight. Telling myself that the contents of this capsule would deliver some entirely new understanding, not only of Sadie, but of us, I lifted the lid and dragged the beam of light—with cinematically slowed motion—across the box's interior. Sadie had painted the inside a bottomless shade of black, which was just one of the reasons why it took me so long to accept what should have been obvious. There was nothing inside.

We did not talk about the trade. The next morning, standing in the hall outside of Miss Meechum's class, I gave Sadie her capsule, and she gave me mine. The school day passed like a school day does, after which I went down to The Pipe, and there was Sadie, playing her guitar.

As soon as I climbed in, Sadie said, "Sit down. I want to play you a song I wrote after looking through your capsule. It's called 'The Boy Who Thought the World Wanted Saving'."

Sadie: What's with the sunglasses?

Me: I don't like eyes.

Sadie: It's true. Eyes are weird. But what specifically creeps you out about them?

Me: I hate how wet and roving they are. I hate how they're always looking at you.

Sadie: Would it make you feel better if I told you that no one is looking at you?

Me: Are you kidding me? I would like someone to tell me that every minute of every day.

Sadie: Well, I'm only going to say it this once. But
        believe me—except for me and maybe your
        mother, no one here is looking at you.
        You're not that interesting. There. You feel
        better now?
Me: I feel incredible.

Eyes had long given me the creeps, and this fear intensified in the move from elementary to middle school. I did not yet know words like "social anxiety" or "introverted personality." All I knew was that wherever I was—the classroom, or the cafeteria, or some scrubby little field built to host a barely enjoyable sport—all proximate eyes seemed aimed, for reasons I couldn't fathom, at me. I hated those eyes. I preferred home, the library, or The Pipe. I preferred to be alone and, if possible, reading. If I had to go out, sunglasses saved me. With those on, I was the watched but also the watcher.

Even in reading my Bible, I was confronted by the sheer weirdness of eyes. Take the scene from the Gospel of Mark where Jesus spat into the eyes of the blind man at Bethsaida. He asked the man, "Do you see anything?" It is reported that the man looked around and, still partially blind, replied, "I see people. They look like trees walking around." Only after Jesus prayed for him a second time did the man fully recover his sight. This repetition is singular. Nowhere else in the Gospels does Jesus have to try twice before delivering a miracle. Why did all other forms of defection—all those crippled legs and possessed minds and even Lazarus who was four days dead and gone—respond so willingly to Christ's first word? Why is the eye the only instrument that demands a double miracle? Anyone who tells you they know the answer to this question is a liar. Anyone who tells you there is no answer is a fool.

"Take those sunglasses off and look me in the eyes!" said Mr. Welsh, who had held me after class to yell at me for turning in a half-finished lab report

"Can't do it, Mr. Welsh," I said.

"Why not?"

"It's too damn weird."

"What did you say?"

I pushed the sunglasses so far up on the bridge of my nose that the plastic cracked against my bone. Mr. Welsh was a harmless gray ghost when seen through the darkened plastic of the shades. I told him, "I said this conversation is making me uncomfortable."

I asked my mother for her theory. "Eyes are the windows to the heart," she told me.

"What are you trying to say?" I replied.

"You're like most of the men I know," she said. "Hearts make you squirm."

I asked my Sadie for her theory. "So what if you don't like eyes?" she said. "Maybe you're more of an ear man."

Here is a true eye story: one night, about a year before the divorce, my family was at the dinner table. One minute: normal family, normal meal. Then I look up and see a face pressed against the bay window behind our table. The face belonged to a white man with bright blue eyes and patches of grey stubble exploding in patches out of his sunken cheeks.

"Dad," I whispered. "Someone's watching us."

Having reported this, I expected my father to get his gun and face the intruder, or for my mother to call the police, or for some kind (any kind!) of terror to be expressed. But what happened was the opposite of terror. It was tranquility.

"Eat your food," my father said. "That's just Mr. Stiles."

My mother was equally unconcerned.

"Don't look at him," she said, spearing a potato with her fork. "He'll be gone in a minute."

He was gone in a minute, but he didn't stay gone. Mr. Stiles reappeared several months later, this time after dinner, to stand at the window and watch us watch TV. He showed up a final time—that is, we noticed him a final time—on Christmas Eve, when he stayed for over an hour while we made a fire, drank hot chocolate, and sang Christmas carols. I had been discouraged from asking about Mr. Stiles. But I remember looking up halfway through "Silent Night."

My mother, who had a voice like Billie Holiday, sang, "All is calm, all is bright."

I wanted to believe this, but as long as those eyes were in the window, I could believe nothing. I struggled simply to breathe.

More and more, Sadie wanted to hang out at her trailer, but her trailer bummed me out, and I told her so.

"It's a trailer," she said. "It's not designed to make you happy."

"It's not that," I said. "It's your mom. What's her deal?"

"I don't know," Sadie said. "She's a lush and a weirdo. She might've been fired from 7-Eleven. Why? Did something happen?"

Something had happened. A couple of days earlier, I had showed up at the trailer hoping to catch Sadie. I knocked on the door, and her mother answered.

The first time I saw Sadie's mother, I thought that she was gorgeous. I thought that she looked like Shania Twain. When I told Sadie this, she laughed and said, "Shania Twain on meth."

"Who are you?" her mother said from behind the screen.

"I'm Sadie's friend," I said. "Is she home?"

"Oh," she said. "You're Sadie's friend."

She came out of the trailer and walked right up to me. For a moment, she stared at me. I knew from her eyes that she was loaded, but I also knew (from Sadie) that she was mostly harmless even when seriously drunk. I looked at my shoes and waited for whatever happened next, and what happened next was not something I intended to share with Sadie.

Without saying anything, her mother danced a weird circle around me—nothing sexual, just alcoholic—and for a full minute, she kept dancing that circle, and she kept saying, "Oh, oh, oh, oh, oh."

Then she stopped dancing, and she pretended to slice open my stomach with an invisible knife.

"Slice!" she said, working her pretend blade from left to right across my abdomen.

She found this hilarious and, pointing to my stomach, began to laugh. Following this, she sliced me in both knees, both ankles, one hip, both wrists, my right eye, and my neck.

"Slice! Slice!" she said. "Slice! Slice! Slice! Slice!"

After the neck slice, she stumbled back and sat on the trailer steps. She leaned back against the door and looked ready to pass out. I started to leave.

"Wait!" she said. "Will you do me a favor?"

"What?"

"Go to the store and get me some cigarettes."

She slipped a moist wad of singles out of her bra and handed them to me. I took the money and told her I would buy the cigarettes, but on the walk to the store, I got so depressed about the whole situation that I went home instead.

I did not think Sadie's mother would remember, but the next time I saw her, she glared at me with those big, beautiful, Shania eyes, and she said, "Where are my smokes, motherfucker?" Before I could answer, there was an invisible knife thrust deep into my heart.

Miss Meechum: Be careful.

Me: Why's that?

Miss Meechum: I've been reviewing your capsule.
      Sadie's taking over.
Me: Of course she is. What else is going on around
      here?
Miss Meechum: Used to be I wouldn't have to
      answer that question. Especially not for
      you.
Me: What are you trying to say?
Miss Meechum: I've already said it. Be careful.

"I agree with your teacher. Fall in love, but don't
disappear." My father.

My mother was still sowing seeds for my soul. Every
night, the prayers. Every morning, the devotionals.
Her message was simple: Jesus loves you; love Him
back. Especially now that the end was near.

"It's not enough to be a seeker," she said. "He calls
you to be a believer."

"I read the Bible everyday," I said. "I go to church
on Sunday, and I try to be kind to everyone I meet.
What's left?"

"Make space for Him," she said. "In your heart."

"Is this about Sadie?" I said. "Are you asking me to
break up with her?"

"No," she said. "I'm asking you to commit."

"I tithe my allowance. I try not to cuss. I pray for people throughout the day, even Rusty Riggins when I remember."

"We are talking about different things."

"What are you talking about?"

"A relationship with Jesus," she said.

I shared my theory about the difference between a believer and a seeker. I thought a shared lexicon would be good for our dialogue.

Her response: "Where do you get this stuff?"

I tapped on the top of my head: "In here."

I ran into Rusty Riggins at the grocery store, in the produce section of all places. He was walking around with his fists balled and partially raised. Two words were etched across his knuckles in dark blue ink. On one fist, it read: K.I.L.L. On the other: L.O.V.E. The symbolism therein interested me about as much as a trip to the dentist.

Rusty: Don't I know you?

Me: Nope.

Rusty: Yeah, I do. I think I beat your ass the other day.

Me: You're thinking of someone else.

Rusty: No way. I know you. You're the shitbird with
      sunglasses and a speech impediment.
Me: Rusty, listen to me. There are two shitbirds with
      sunglasses and a speech impediment. You're
      thinking of the other one.
I grabbed a jazz apple and went my own way.

You can be in love and still need your space. When the itch to be alone got bad enough, I faked sick. Such as yesterday, when I said my stomach hurt, and my mother believed me, and Sadie believed me, and I was left alone in a house as quiet as a monastery. This allowed me to spend the entire day in bed reading. I seized this quiet to build a cave out of my covers. I crawled down into it, and in the muted blue light, I read about half of *The Selected Poems of E.E. Cummings*, which is more than enough to send you spiraling off into the best weird dream you have ever had.

This day was so good that when my mother came home that evening and checked on me, I stayed in the cave and pretended to be asleep. Even when she sat on the bed and called my name, even when she reached down and placed her hand on my forehead, I kept my eyes closed. I felt secure in the knowledge that no one could see through this performance.

The next morning, my mother asked if I felt good enough to go to school. I had already built the cave and supplied its base with snacks, a flashlight, and a copy of *The Illustrated New Testament*. I looked her straight in her eyes and said, "Absolutely not. I'm even worse than yesterday."

Most days, when school let out, Sadie and I went directly to The Pipe. Sometimes, though, I ditched her and snuck off to the library. I never told anyone I was going, and when I got back, I would lie about where I had been. Sometimes I would stay there and not even read. I would just hold a book in my hands and lay out on the couch. Barry was there and so was the light. G.G. was next door, a million miles away. It was not a library. It was an island.

I did not tell Sadie about the library. For one, she wasn't a serious reader. For two, I liked the idea of having one place that no one else could claim. Too many secrets makes you paranoid. Just one made you powerful.

"People in Carolina are phonies," Sadie said. "All the

fake smiles. All the bullshit stories. What the hell is going on here?"

"I don't know," I said. "I was born here, and I've never left."

"Well it's not this way everywhere. It's definitely not this way in Florida."

"How is it?"

"In Florida," she said. "You tell the truth. Even if it hurts. Especially if it hurts."

"You sound like someone with a low view of humanity."

"You sound like someone from Carolina."

I called my father and told him what Sadie said. I asked him, "Do you think people from Carolina are phonies?"

He muted the television, which was the ultimate sign that a topic had seized his interest. He took a sip of his beer and said, "I had a fraternity brother at Clemson who used to fake a limp and tell girls he was wounded in the war. He got a lot of mileage out of that story."

"Was he not in the war?"

"He wasn't even in the military."

I was thinking about this—about how anyone can tell any story at any time and stand the chance, however slight, of pulling off a mirage—when my dad drove his point home.

"I've known Southern women who pretend to be sexy because they want to be loved. I've known Southern men who pretend to be loving because they don't want to be lonely. I knew a boy from Greer who was so ashamed of his region that he neutralized his accent and told everyone he was from Iowa. To tell you the truth, though, I think this kind of thing goes on everywhere."

"Why would it?"

"Because reality gets boring, and sometimes we need more."

Here is a question I put to Sadie. I said, "You think Florida is weirder than Carolina?"

"Of course it is," she said. "It's not even close."

So I told her about the annual grits festival (held a couple counties over) where people literally swim in vats of hot grits. Then I told her about the state fair, where I saw an eight-hundred-pound woman dance the shag with an albino dwarf. I told her about the flea markets and the jockey lots, the Lost Cause and the Daughters of the Confederacy, the Lizard Man over in Bishopville and the Grey Man down in Charleston, our pride of Shoeless Joe Jackson and our shame over Pee Wee Gaskins. I told her about the catacombs under Columbia, the moonshine set ups in Anderson, the abandoned castle at Heritage USA in Fort Hill, the island of wild monkeys in Beaufort, the tanning yards in Spartanburg, and the countless churches spread out across the state.

I submitted everything I had, half of which came from stories my father told me, and when I was finished, Sadie sucked her teeth and said, "Small potatoes."

"We have Rusty Riggins," I said.

"Rusty Riggins wouldn't last a day in Florida."

I asked my father for a story about the biggest phony he knew. He told a story about a girl from his hometown who was known for her seriousness. She had a serious face and a serious voice and, whenever she started talking about her "convictions," she let you know how deadly serious the stakes were.

Years later, she became locally famous for starting a center for battered women and for writing a best-selling book titled *Hands Off: The Hidden Truth About Domestic Violence*. She was all over television (still very serious), and she was telling the story of her first marriage, wherein her husband would tie her to the bed and beat her with a phonebook.

She looked into the camera and, with tears streaming down her cheeks, she said, "Maybe you're watching this, and you're in a relationship where someone is abusing you. And maybe you think that you're trapped, and that there's no hope for you. Well, there is hope. Call the number at the bottom of this screen, and one of our trained specialists will give you information on the next step to freedom."

About five years after that, she became even more famous. She was arrested, along with her new husband, for running a prostitution ring out of the battered women's shelter. Many women came forward with troubling stories and eventually she was charged with solicitation. She served two years in prison, where she became a born-again Christian. Once released, she started a new ministry (a counseling center) and published another book (*Prodigal Soul: Seven Secrets to Revitalizing Your Faith*).

My father pointed her out on a late night infomercial, where she wept again in the course of promoting her book. She was thin and well-dressed. Her seriousness was intact.

Rusty Riggins brought a knife to school. They let him off with a day of in-school suspension because he said it was never his intention to kill anyone. He said he only wanted to scare a few mouthy Ohioans, and the consensus from the students was "At least it wasn't a gun."

The world was inviting me to think more about death. This past Saturday, for instance. It was morning and I put down the assignment in order to ride my bike to Wilson's Five and Dime. When I stepped outside, it was seventy-seven degrees with blue skies, green grass, et cetera. It was the kind of morning so perfect that it makes you stop and think, "Maybe the world is not limping toward its end. Maybe all anyone needs is a bit of sun." I was thinking this and rolling down my driveway when I saw something lying in the street. I got closer and saw it was a pup. The yellow fur, the cream belly. The floppy ears, the limp tail. I got closer and saw the pup was dead. To make sure, I found a stick and poked its leg. Before the stick, I could have told myself (and half-believed), "It's only sleeping."

I swung by the library and noticed that Barry was no longer holding *The Waste Land*. Instead, his bony hands had been taped to a book titled *The Top 100 Unusual Deaths In History*. I borrowed the book and started to read, beginning with the early Christians.

According to the author, only one of Jesus's twelve disciples died of natural causes (John the Revelator, old age). The Apostle Paul was captured and decapitated by Nero. Thomas was stabbed with spears. Bleak as these are, here are the worst:

Simon the Zealot, who was tied to posts in Persia and sawn in half

Peter, who was hung on a cross upside down

James, son of Alphaeus, who was pushed off the roof of a temple then stoned

There was another book in the library that covered myths and misunderstandings about death.

Apparently, your hair and fingernails do not continue to grow even after you die. What happens is an optical illusion: the flesh (dehydrated) shrinks back, giving the appearance of increased length.

Later, I called my father and told him about the dog.

Me: I know death happens. It's everywhere. It's inevitable. Even still, it gets me down.

My father: I know. Me too. I've been that way since I was young, which means you'll probably be that way until you're old like me.

Me: So you never stop thinking about it?

My father: Nope.

Me: And it never stops making you sad?

My father: Nope.

Me: But it's everywhere. How do you know it's
      there and keep moving forward? How do
      you not go crazy?

My father: You like analogies. Try this one: you're
      in an elevator with strangers.

Me: Okay.

My father: And the doors have closed. And the
      buttons have been pushed. And you're
      standing there, sharing this space with
      folks you'll never know. It's so quiet, and
      it's so weird, and everyone's just standing
      there and praying the thing will start to
      move. Only it doesn't. There is absolutely
      no movement. Oh, and it's hot too.

Me: Okay.

My father: And then, standing there in the perfect
      quiet and the growing heat, it hits you.

Me: Someone farted?

My father: You got it. They dropped a bomb.
      Except that this is the worst one you have
      ever smelled in your life. You smell it, and
      everyone else smells it, and it makes the sad
      and weird situation infinitely more sad and
      more weird. And yet, what do you say?

Me: What can you say? Nothing. You stand there
      and wait for the elevator to move.
My father: Exactly. That's life, and that's death.
      At least in Carolina it is.
Me: Can I ask you one more question about
      death?
My father: No.

Northwoods Middle drilled us for a variety of
future deaths. Fire drill! Fire drill! Line up! File out!
Remember the evacuation route that we discussed!
We have to practice, practice, practice! This is a drill,
but fires do happen! Your life might depend on your
ability to listen!

First a dog, then a deer. A buck with big black eyes.
This was on a walk to Sadie's trailer. Its guts had been
spilled, and the flies were horrendous. I had to cross
to the other side of the street. I had to find a song to
hum, and strongarm my mind not to drift back to the
site. Something was coming, and it let me feel it creep-
ing closer. I lowered my voice to the level of Elvis's
and whispered, "Time goes by so slowly. And time
can do so much. Are you still mine?"

Tornado drill! Tornado drill! Out into the hall! Down on the floor! Now cover your head with your arms and be quiet until further notice! I don't want to see anyone's face popping up to look around! You'll survive this wind if you move fast and get low!

The worst death was the one that only half killed you. Take Thomas Shepherd. Back in elementary school, Thomas finished first in everything regardless of subject. Every science project, every spelling bee, every art exhibit, or math competition—there was Thomas with his smart little face, and his smart little clothes, and with that subtle, awkward smile that seemed to say to us, "Shucks, y'all, I never meant to make it look this easy."

Thomas Shepherd was so smart that Miss Leeland called him "Einstein," after which everyone called him "Einstein."

On Career Day, when the rest of us laid out our dreams of becoming teachers and pastry chefs and police officers, Einstein said, "I'm going to be a neurosurgeon." Since no one knew what a neurosurgeon was, Einstein had to explain it, in addition to explaining how, to become a neurosurgeon, one had to complete four years of undergraduate work, four years of medical school, and seven years of residency.

He said, "That's fifteen years in all, and not many people make it all the way through. But I will. I will make it because I know I was put on this earth to be a neurosurgeon." He reported this with much confidence but not an ounce of arrogance. We believed him.

From first grade through fourth grade, you saw Einstein acing his tests and racking up his awards, and you thought, "There's our guy. One day he's going to be a neurosurgeon, but for now, he's here, and I know him." It gave you such pride to know that a guy like Einstein could emerge from your state, which ranked forty-eighth in education.

Then came the accident. The details were fuzzy and, in the sense that time cannot be reversed, insignificant. Einstein was at his cousin's (or uncle's) house, and he was riding a dirt bike (or four-wheeler), and he fell (or was pushed off), and he landed on his head. This last detail is the only detail that matters, since the fall caused bleeding, and the bleeding caused brain damage, and by the time Einstein returned to school, he was no longer the boy who was perfect at everything.

After his accident, Einstein was placed into special education classes, which were held in the basement of our school, and which no one from the larger student body would ever see, unless they made a special trip down to that level. I did make a special trip but only once, since what I witnessed was too sad to see again.

I told Miss Leeland that I had to use the restroom, then I took the stairwell down to the basement, which was dark and smelled weirdly of oranges. I snuck over to the slim pane of glass that looked into the special education classroom.

There was one teacher in the room, a fat woman in her sixties with an angry face, and she was at her desk reading a *National Inquirer*. The students were seated at small, round tables that were covered in crayons, puzzles, and what looked to be toy blocks. Some of the students were coloring or playing with the blocks, but most of them were sleeping.

Einstein sat alone at a table in the corner. There were crayons and blocks on his table, but he paid them no attention. He sat in his chair with his arms flat at his side, and with his head tilted forward, and with his mouth hanging open so that a thin ribbon of saliva looped down his chin. He appeared to be staring at something, but I could not tell what. The wall in front of him was the color of oatmeal, and it was void of any posters.

Cued by some invisible force, Einstein stopped looking at the wall and snapped his face directly toward the window where I watched. He looked at me, and I looked back at him, and although everything else about him looked different, his eyes were the same as before the accident. They were smart and hungry eyes, *too* smart and *too* hungry for the rest of the simple face. They were like two scared creatures taking refuge in the rubble of a bombed-out building.

Possibly because I was young, but probably because I was a coward, I ran out of the basement and returned to class. Everyone still calls him Einstein. I have wondered if he answers to it.

It did not matter that the year was nearly over, and it did not matter that everyone (even the students) sensed she would be fired if she did not quit the assignment and return to the curriculum—Miss Meechum remained committed. Lately, she was keen on the idea of half-page essays to be written, folded up as origami animals, and stored amongst the artifacts. She walked to the chalkboard and wrote, "If you could have any superpower, what would it be, and what would you do with it?"

We wrote for a while in silence, after which Miss Meechum asked if anyone wanted to share their response.

The second prettiest girl in school stood up and read, "If I could have any superpower, I would have the power of flight."

She described how this ability would allow her to commune with birds and, if necessary, retrieve objects that were stuck in high places.

A football player named Jaxton went next.

"I want super strength," he said. "I want to be able to pick up cars and throw them like they're footballs. I would use this power to punch the ground and cause an earthquake. Also to play in the NFL and catch bad guys who won't surrender."

My response, which I folded into the shape of an ivory-billed woodpecker and shared only with Sadie, ran thus: "Freeze time."

Sadie (on the phone one night): Why do you want to freeze time?

Me: Because I don't want to die. I don't want anyone to die. I want all of us and all of this to stay. Forever, if possible.

Sadie: Be careful.

Me: Why's that?

Sadie: Because. You're falling in love again.

Me: It's true. But you know me. That's kind of my move.

Sadie: Well, put this moment in your shoebox. It's the one where I told you to find a new move.

Here are the Scriptures my mother read to me when I told her about the dog, and the deer, and the sense that a more deadly form of death was right around the corner. Take note of the last one, which played a part in getting me through some long nights.

"For since we believe that Jesus died and rose again, even so, through Jesus, God will bring with him those who have fallen asleep." 1 Thessalonians 4:14.

"For if we live, we live to the Lord, and if we die, we die to the Lord. So then, whether we live or whether we die, we are the Lord's." Romans 14:8.

"He will wipe away every tear from their eyes, and death shall be no more, neither shall there be mourning, nor crying, nor pain anymore, for the former things have passed away." Revelation 21:4.

Here is a "former thing" I want frozen for all of time: when Sadie kissed me, I could smell the glue in her hair. She used Elmer's. It was the kind that comes in the white bottle with the orange cap.

I need you to accept this copy of *London Calling* by

The Clash, and here is why. One night, Sadie showed up at The Pipe with this album and a six pack of beer. My mother was working a double, which granted us impunity. Sadie drank four, and I drank two, and we felt immensely good in our secret, underground buzz. She straddled me and put her big red headphones on my ears. She said, "Enough about death. Here is some medicine."

I listened. It was "Lost in the Supermarket" by The Clash.

When the song ended, she said, "How did that make you feel?"

"Sad," I said. "But, at the same time, honest."

She said, "What was your favorite line?"

I said, "The one where he talked about the hedge in the suburbs that he couldn't see over."

"That's a good one," she said, "But I like it when he sings, 'I empty a bottle, I feel a bit free.'"

Later, at her trailer, we drank some more beer, and we watched a VHS compilation of music videos, live performances, and interviews with The Clash.

"That's Joe Strummer," Sadie said. "If he says something, you can believe that it's true."

I looked at the man on the screen. He had an orange mohawk and a black leather jacket, but he had the sad eyes of a local librarian. He looked like someone I could believe in.

This was the same night I got drunk enough to say it for the first (and only) time: "Hey, Sadie?"

"Yeah."

"I love you."

"Hey, Junah?"

"Yeah?"

"Go get us some more beer."

Earthquake drill! Earthquake drill! Get away from the windows! Get under your desks! Hang on to something stable! It is going to seem like the world is ending, but this will all be over soon!

Me: What happens after death?

Miss Meechum: Can't say. Never been there.

Me: Do you have a guess?

Miss Meechum: Nope.

Me: What about a hope?

Miss Meechum: An eternity of this would be nice.

Me: Sadie said an eternity of this would get boring.

Miss Meechum: Tell Sadie only boring people get bored.

Probably because of my Christian upbringing, I expected a bit of death to be built into a serious gesture of love. Consider this newspaper clipping, which features a man from our hometown on the front page. He had cheated on his wife, and she had left him. But he loved her, and he asked her what he could do to get her back. She said, "Crawl." He took this literally. He cut up one of his tires and taped the strips of tread to his hands and knees. Using these paws, he crawled seven miles across our town to the motel where his wife was staying. It was summer, ninety-six degrees. So many people saw him and reported it that the news stations sent out their cameras.

"Sir," said one of the reporters. "Why are you doing this?"

Still on his hands and knees, the man looked up and stared directly into the camera. He was sunburned and dripping with sweat.

"This is for you, Jade," he said. "I love you, and I'm sorry."

He continued crawling, and they continued filming. It took him all day to get to the motel, and everyone who had been following the story was eager to see if the wife would take him back. But when he got to the motel, his wife was gone. She had watched the story along with the rest of our town, but about halfway through his journey, she had hopped in her car and driven to her sister's house in Spartanburg.

She had the decency to leave him a note. The

reporters read it aloud as he sat there on the motel porch and picked bits of dirty tread out of his fingers. It was a single sentence: "I don't believe you."

I thought the story about the man crawling across town on paws made of tread was inspirational. Sadie thought it was stupid. I reported this to my father one night on the phone. I said, "She sees it one way, I see it another, and that's fine. There's a danger in making too much of interpretive differences." His reply: "Isn't there a danger in making too little?"

Joe Strummer knew something. He was punk and very alive, and he might have been a prophet. But give me fat and dying Elvis any day of the week. Broken people need broken heroes.

Me: Was Elvis punk?
   Sadie: No. He was iconic, and, occasionally, he
             was good. But he never came close to being
             punk.
Me: You ever seen the concert where Elvis sings
             "Unchained Melody"? It was filmed like
             two weeks before he died. And you can tell
             that he's dying from how bloated and tired

and sad he looks. And you can tell he knows he's dying. And even though he knows it's almost over, he's smiling that smile, and he's singing like maybe it'll be okay.

Sadie: What's your point?

Me: Singing a love song into death's face seems pretty punk to me.

Sadie: I'll give you that one.

You will have guessed by now that all of this, the minor hits and theoreticals, was warm up for the big one, for that day in late November when Coach Mac stood in front of the class and said, "Good morning. I'm afraid I have some tragic news. Rusty Riggins is no longer with us."

That was all Coach Mac could manage. He put his big, hairy hands over his face and wept. Then the girls in the room wept. Then the boys.

Eventually a hand went up, and someone asked how he died.

"He drowned," said Coach Mac.

"In a pool?"

"At the beach."

That was it, and for the next few minutes, the school was as quiet as it had ever been. It felt cowardly to be so quiet. And yet, whenever you tried to put your

feelings into words, that felt even worse. Like reaching out for words that belonged to a language you
didn't speak, or trying to hold the ocean in the palm
of your hand.

"It happens," Sadie said. "Move forward."
"No."
"Rusty was an asshole."
"Irrelevant."
"Come December, we'll all be gone anyway."
"I believe otherwise."

If there is a genre of grief, it is lists. We know everything must end, but we don't know what (if anything)
follows us to the other side. Lists collect what we
would take if given the chance. "This is it," a good
list says. "My essentials."

Top three Rusty Riggins memories.
Three: the time in third grade when he pulled the
fire alarm that forced Miss Leeland to reschedule (and
eventually cancel) our spelling test.
Two: the time in first grade when he forged Ken

Griffey Jr.'s autograph onto a bucket of baseballs and sold them for twenty dollars apiece.

One: the time in fifth grade when I caught him crying in the alley behind the YMCA. He was kicking a dumpster and screaming as if in pain.

"Hey, Rusty," I said. "Are you okay?"

When he realized he was not alone, he turned away. He wiped his eyes and spit hard onto the pavement. When he turned back around, he tried to fake the toughness of the old Rusty, except that he failed. I could see in his eyes he was hurt.

"Come any closer," he said. "And I'll kick your ass."

"What's going on, Rusty?"

"Fuck you."

"Okay," I said. "But seriously, Rusty, what's going on?"

Instead of answering this, he lifted up his shirt. Bruises darker and larger than any I had ever seen covered Rusty's midsection.

"Your stepdad?" I said.

"No," he said. "My mom."

He lowered his shirt, and we sat there in the alley for a long time and said nothing to each other. When we did speak, it would be the last thing we said to each other for a very long time.

"If you ever tell anyone about this," he said. "I'll murder you."

"Okay," I said. "I promise."

"I just turned twelve," he said. "Did you know that a minor in South Carolina can be emancipated at fifteen?"

That fact had never crossed my mind.

On the day they told us that Rusty Riggins was dead, the teachers canceled classes and sent us home. They were right to do this, since we had no space left in our heads for their subjects. A kid was dead—a kid who we knew, and a kid who could have been us—and for the rest of that day, that fact took up all the space there was.

It was two miles to my house, and I covered it alone and in a trance, stumbling past the familiar scenery and thinking not so much about Rusty's death as about his dying. Somehow I ended up in the back of a Wilson's Five and Dime, where my entire body felt frozen and numb, and where I stared at a rack of candies until the old clerk slapped me on the back and said, "Shit or get off the pot, son."

From the neck down, I was still frozen, yet my head swiveled to look this man in his eyes. He was famous in our town for three things: his loyalty to the

Republican party, his vicious and far-reaching halito-sis, and his eternal suspicion that every kid who came into his store was a shoplifter. I had been in Wilson's many times before. Never once had he offered to help me.

"What's it going to be?" he said and seemed to be pushing me out of his store with his shitty breath.

"I'm thinking," I said and turned back to the candies.

My eyes fell on a fat bag of black licorice. It was the old-fashioned kind that comes in little tightly wound wheels. I was staring at those shiny black wheels when the old man slapped me on the back a second time.

"Go to a library if you want to think," he said. "I run a store."

With this, the man moved closer. He was so close I could feel his breath on the top of my head. I knew he was looking at me, but I was still looking at the licorice. If you looked at those wheels long enough, they stopped looking like wheels and started look-ing like mouths. That man could stare at me all day long, I didn't care. I was looking at a bag of shiny black mouths all thrown open in perfect circles so as to scream, "Help me! Help me! I'm drowning over here!"

The old man clasped his bony hands onto my shoul-ders and cleared his throat. He leaned down and whispered, "Listen, you seem like a good kid. I'd hate to have to call the cops."

"Cops" was the word that snapped the spell. When he said, "Cops," my arm shot out and snatched the licorice, my head swung itself back and slammed into the old man's chin, and my feet moved faster than ever before, carrying me out of Wilson's and flinging me into the light.

Outside, I did not stop running. The old man was back there screaming something, but it was a mousy nothing compared with the blood thumping in my ears. I ran until his voice could no longer reach me, until sweat covered everything, until I was falling down and sputtering in the kudzu behind The Pipe.

In the final days of November, I could not stop looking at Rusty's desk, and whenever I did, I found myself facing a minor kind of magic. Instead of seeing the place where he was not, I saw the place where he was supposed to be. I saw, not Rusty, but Rusty's silhouette, his shadow, a strange vapor too stubborn to dissipate.

I had experienced this feeling once before, in response to a painting that used to hang on the wall above our kitchen table. It was a watercolor that featured an old stone well in the middle of an empty field. It was a sad little painting, and I had no idea why my mother liked it, since it had been there since before I was born, but every morning at breakfast, and every night at dinner, and about a million other times in the course of my days, I would stare at that painting, in particular the well, and I would feel some deep sense of being safe and at home. I loved the painting and memorized every color and every texture of the well and the field and the evening light that was breaking through the treeline. But one day I looked up, and the painting was gone. My mother, who apparently had never cared for the watercolor, had plucked it off the wall on a whim and thrown it away, leaving a faded rectangle of emptiness on the wall. It was gone, but sometimes I still saw it. Sometimes, I had to remind myself what happened.

If Rusty's desk and my mother's watercolor taught me anything, it was this: dying is not the same as disappearing. Your eyes say to the dead, "I can't see you, which means you're gone." But your heart has the last word, and it replies, "I believe otherwise."

On the last day of November, as we made our daily adjustments to the capsules, I asked Miss Meechum a question that had troubled me for years. Well before Rusty died. Well before the world got obsessed with death by computers. I asked her, "If my capsule is supposed to contain memories, do I have to remember things exactly as they happened?"

Miss Meechum thought about this for a moment. (She was always doing that—*thinking* about your questions as if they were on par with the world's true concerns.)

"There are people who think memory is connected to accuracy," she said. "These people believe categories. Fiction starts here, nonfiction is over there. This is a work of fantasy, but that is a work of truth. They are quite serious, these categorists."

"Are you a categorist?"

"No," she said. "And neither are you."

"Is there a limit to what I can change?"

"If there is," she said. "I'm not the one who can show it to you."

Later that night, I removed from my capsule all evidence of Rusty's death—the obituary, the funeral program, any writing of mine that referenced his passing. In the space opened up by these subtractions, I deposited this note: "*Here is a true story. Rusty Riggins was swimming in the ocean when he drowned. He went out too far and couldn't come back. Good news, though: there was a lifeguard on duty who saw this and saved him. Rusty was back at school today, and he told us it was like the movies. The CPR in the sand. The coughing up of saltwater. Everyone cheering as Rusty sat up and took his first sweet and sputtering breaths of oxygen. Rusty smiled the whole time he told this story. He said, 'Death thought he could take me, but I punched a hole through his ass.'"*

Here is a true story, and I urge you to believe it: Rusty Riggins is alive.

December 1999

IT'S TRUE: DECEMBER found me frantic. I don't know if it was losing Rusty, or if it was the thought of losing everyone, but I felt itchy in my need to store up existence.

Me (faux confident): "Miss Meechum, my time capsule's full. Can I have another one?"

Miss Meechum (truly confused): "If it's full, then you've completed the assignment."

Me (insistent): "Sure, but can I complete a couple more?"

Miss Meechum (intrigued): "Why would you want to do that?"

Me (nervous): "There's so many stories worth
    saving. I hate the thought of losing them,
    you know?"
Miss Meechum (nervous): "This is about Rusty,
    isn't it? You know, Junah, grief is a—"
Me (exiting her room): "Nevermind. I'll find my
    own shoebox."

I found my own shoebox and filled it. Then I found another one and filled it too. By the second week of December, I had six different capsules. Sometimes each box contained its own arrangement, and each one felt like its own delicate ecosystem. Sometimes I would empty all of them onto the floor of my bedroom so as to kick the memories around like a pile of dead leaves.

Dead leaf no. 72: an old matchbook from my father's glove compartment that features, on one side, a naked blonde holding a beer stein and an assault rifle, and on the other side, the words BIG JUICY'S. If I knew the story, I would tell it here. For this one, though, we are both flying blind.

Sadie knew the score.

"You're afraid to die," she said. "That's why you're trying so hard to hold on to everything."

"You must know a better way."

"I do," she said. "It's called letting go."

I laughed so hard I nearly pissed myself. Letting go? Sadie knew everything about everything, but she still didn't know the first thing about me.

Here is something that only happened once.

"Sadie's right," my mother said. "The harder you try to hold onto things in this world, the more your heart breaks when they're gone."

"What's the alternative? Love people and things, but don't get so attached?"

"Exactly."

"I've considered that strategy," I told her. "It interests me about as much as suicide."

The masters of nonattachment were kids from out of state. Because I had been staring at Carolinians since preschool, these outsiders made for a welcome break in the tedium. They would wear a different brand of jeans, or they would have a weird haircut, or they'd pronounce a word in a strange way ("roof" so as to

rhyme with "hoof" or "wash" with "r" sound in it).
Sometimes they'd wear a sweatshirt for a sports team
I never knew existed. The differences were there (if
you cared to spot them), but all their backstories were
minor variations of the same pattern.

"What brought you down here?" some local kid
would ask.

"My dad," the outsider would reply. "He's
military."

"What branch?"

"Army."

"You got a girlfriend?"

"Of course."

"Down here?"

"No. Back home."

"You like it here?"

To which they'd give a requisite shrug meant to
convey an ambivalence located somewhere between
"I don't know" and "Sure, whatever."

Then came the time for the most pointless question
of all. It was pointless, but some local kid asked it
anyway: "Where are you from originally?"

They never answered with a specific town, and
they never answered with "All over the place."
They always looked down at the ground and said,
"Nowhere." After which they might rattle off a list
of cities whose names meant nothing more to you

than a page of strangers torn out of a phonebook: Columbus, Montgomery, Tucson, Sacramento, Aurora, Brevard, Fort Worth, Marietta, Des Moines, Brunswick, Bedford, Pascagoula, and Fairview.

No one got attached to these kids from Nowhere because they'd never stick around for more than a year or two. They knew this and acted accordingly, isolating at recess and declining all invitations to try out for a sports team or join a youth group. They were content to exist in Carolina as long as their dad's service demanded, after which time they would leave town without a single goodbye and thereafter be known as "That kid from Texas with the big ears" or "What's-her-name from Jersey who was kind of cute and had the birthmark on her cheek." They were Nobodies from Nowhere, unlike those of who were born in Carolina, and who would die in Carolina, and who therefore carried the silly weight of being Somebody from Somewhere.

Our lives said, "Look over here! Remember this! Remember me!"

Nobodies didn't have it easier, but they did have it lighter.

"Relax," their every action whispered. "In a couple of years, you will have forgotten me, and I will have forgotten you. Treat this like a dream. It'll die soon enough."

I was born in South Carolina. I will die in South Carolina. This is it—my beginning, middle, and end—so be careful when you tell me to not get attached.

You will wonder, "What is with all these tiny balls of paper?" I can explain. When Sadie got bored in class, she would write the lyrics of her favorite punk songs onto little strips of paper. Then she would compress these strips into tightly mashed balls and chuck them across the room to me. I remember the first one she sent me. Coach Mac was up at the board carrying on about the crime of misplaced modifiers when—*poomph*!—a tiny paper pill landed directly in my lap.

I opened it up and read: "*You're looking around for someone to love, so you don't have to face the world alone. But give it some time, and you might find that you're better off on your own.*" Beneath this: "*The Descendents.*"

I think this was her way of saying, "It's okay to feel lonely." But it's possible that this message had nothing to do with loneliness, or, for that matter, me. It's possible that Sadie's theme was more along the lines of, "It's almost time for me to leave. Don't say I didn't warn you."

One day, after school, I lined up all my capsules in The Pipe. I was up to ten, and it thrilled me to see how full each box was. When Sadie saw them, she shook her head and said, "Okay, Pharaoh."

"How's that?"

"You think stuffing a grave with the shit you love makes it feel less like death."

I could tell from the look on Sadie's face that she intended this as an insult and that she expected me to push back. But when I thought about it, I remembered what Miss Meechum had said: "We write because we want to live forever."

So I told Sadie to come with me.

"Where are we going?" she said.

"I need another box."

Miss Meechum: I reviewed your assignment.

Me: And?

Miss Meechum: Give me something where you
don't come out looking like the good guy.

Per Miss Meechum's request: one day I was coming back from the library, and I cut through the parking lot of an abandoned movie theatre, and I found a dirty sleeping bag and, inside it, two bags of chips, a

Ziplock full of pennies, and a *Penthouse* magazine. I looked around. The parking lot was empty. I wanted to be Christ-like and return the magazine to the sleeping bag. I also wanted to see what was inside.

I held the *Penthouse* by its spine, and (applying the same trick I used with the Bible) I let the pages fall away to either side until the magazine had opened itself, under the sovereignty of smooth invisible fingers, to a place predestined for this very moment. I opened my eyes and saw a red-headed woman dressed like a librarian. She was squatting on a table full of books, legs spread so as to pull aside her black-lace panties and expose herself. I tore the page out, folded it in quarters, and slipped it into my sock.

When I came home that night, I intended to report directly to my room, directly to the bookshelves, where I would remove Volume L of my father's old leather-bound *Encyclopedia Britannicas* and hide the librarian deep within those yellowed pages where no one (certainly not him) ever looked.

I was halfway up the stairs when my mother, who was in the kitchen, called my name.

"Come down here," she said.

I turned around and walked into the kitchen, where my mother was seated at the table. Her eyes said she already knew everything. The folded page in my sock burnt against my ankle with a dull heat.

"Sit down," she said and nodded toward the seat across from hers.

I obeyed. She extended her hand across the table, palm up, expectant.

"Give it to me," she said.

"Give you what?"

Nothing in my mother moved. Not her hand, and not her eyes, and not even her voice, as she said, "You know what."

I removed the page from my sock and placed it in her hand. By no design of mine, the fold had left only one thing visible, and that was the books. Then a miracle: my mother crushed the page in her fist then threw it so that it bounced off my chest and landed between us on the table.

"Dinner's ready," my mother said. "Get clean."

In some of my capsules, I am a short kid with a speech impediment who can't face the world without a pair of sunglasses. In others, I am tall and confident, and I speak with the voice of Elvis to win friends and make memories. Just as I have had to imagine many versions of you, you must do the same with me. Don't search for the real me. Accept what's offered. Plumb the subtext.

"Show me the difference between fiction and truth, and I'll show you the difference between a rock and a stone. The question is not, 'What happened?' The question is, 'What do you need to have happened?'"
—Miss Meechum

"Be careful," said Coach Mac. "You lose yourself in writing, next thing you know, you've lost yourself for good."

"That doesn't sound so bad."

"It is," he said. "The truth is all we have."

True to the incorrigible rhythms of Carolina, autumn began feeling like autumn on its own time. Eventually, though, the heat lifted, the foliage darkened, and everything took on a Monet kind of magic, especially in the muted light of evenings.

"I love this," I said to Sadie on a long walk home in which we intentionally stuck to the gutters so as to crunch down the avenue of dead leaves.

"Love it while it lasts," she said. "It's already almost gone."

Sadie's notes helped me through, so I attempted reciprocation. One day during Miss Meechum's class, I wrote my favorite line from The Dead Milkmen's "Punk Rock Girl" on a strip of paper. Then I balled it up and threw it across the room, where it landed in the center of Sadie's desk. She stared at it for about five seconds, then she picked it up, popped it into her mouth, and swallowed it. The only time during that entire class that she looked at me was right after eating the paper. She showed me her long pink tongue as if to prove that it was gone.

Miss Meechum asked me to stay after school. She asked how the assignment was going.

"It's hard to say," I told her.

"Why's that?"

"My mother thinks I'm insane. Sadie thinks I'm unpunk. All I want to do is work on this assignment, but no one gets what I'm doing, so I have to sneak around and arrange stuff in secret. It's starting to feel like I'm doing something illegal."

Mrs. Meechum smiled when I said this.

"That's how you know the work is good," she said. "When it stops feeling safe."

I've included another story written for Coach Mac's class. Since the one about a wolf earned an A, I attempted something similar and wrote a story about a hunter who succeeds in killing the last remainder of a nearly extinct breed of tigers. It was titled "This Machine Kills Futures," and it earned a D. When I asked why, Coach said, "You're projecting."

"Okay," I said, "Do you have any tips on how to improve it?"

"Yeah," Coach said. "Stop projecting."

After referring to a dictionary, an encyclopedia, and a psychology textbook, none of which could rescue "projection" out of watery abstraction, I asked my father for his definition.

"Projection?" he said. "Is that Freud?"

"Who's Freud?"

"Another guy with thoughts about thoughts."

"What does Freud say about projection?"

"Can't say. He's one of so many I should've read when I had the chance. I'm sorry about that, son. I know you're disappointed in me."

This was untrue, and I told him so, but it was no use. When my father committed to a feeling, he went all the way.

"You're disappointed, and that's fine. I'd be

disappointed, too, if I had someone like me for a father."

"I'm not," I said. "I promise."

"You are. And you have every right. I've left you with many stories but not enough ideas. And trust me, son, it's the ideas that save you."

Weekends we spent at The Pipe. The world outside: everything you're used to, only hidden under so many blankets of red and yellow and brown leaves, all dead and all much better than when they were alive. Inside: you hold each other and whisper (even though no one else is around). It was here that Sadie opted for candor.

"I'm not going to warn you again," she said. "Don't get attached to me."

"Why? Is it because you are actually getting attached to me? Are you projecting?"

"You wish. It's just that I may not be around much longer."

"What is that supposed to mean?"

"My mom says they're raising the rent for the new year."

"What are you telling me here?"

"It's not your fault," she said. "It's no one's fault."

"What's not my fault?"

Sadie grabbed her guitar and walked out of The Pipe. Her footsteps snapped twigs as she cut through the woods. She didn't say, "The end is almost here." She didn't have to.

Later, after Sadie had gone home, I lay on my back in the leaves and, waving my arms and legs, created an angel on the ground. Then I stood up and kicked the angel in its head. I gave it a few extra stomps, even after it had lost its form and blended back into the brown rest of the fallen leaves. "Don't worry," I told it. "It's not your fault."

"I think I'm going to lose Sadie," I told my dad that night on the phone.

I knew from the background noise (mainly the voice of Dean Martin but also that clinking of ice on glass and the pop of burning cedar) that he was drinking in front of his fireplace. I knew from the steady string of little slurps that he was drinking his favorite whiskey.

"Can you stop her?" he said.

"No," I said. "It'll happen or it won't."

"Then enjoy it until it does," he said. "Love is like death. Think too much about how it ends, and you'll ruin the middle."

"Sadie's leaving," I told my dad several nights later. "Any day now. I can feel it."

I knew from the background noise that he was propped up in his big chair, watching a documentary on the Civil War. As such, he gave half his attention to me and half his attention to the film.

"That so?" he said.

"Yes," I said. "I would cut off my arm if it meant she would stay."

"Listen kid," he said. "No one wants your arm."

End of conversation. Sometimes your father is a well-timed miracle of insight. Sometimes he is another dude trying to make it through the day. You can't have one without the other.

"Some of this comes back to Rusty. After someone dies, you realize you can lose anyone at anytime. That's how grief works. It ruins the illusion of security." —My mother

"You're all going to have your hearts smashed at some point. You and you and you and you. Even you, back there. Yes, you." —Coach Mac

Like countless other losers and fools, I had it in my head that the perfect gift would procure for Sadie and I some perfectly untouchable future. Such as the guitar in the window of our local music shop, a Gretsch Hollowbody nearly identical to the one that Tim Armstrong played, a charcoal and gold beauty that would've looked immaculate in Sadie's hands. Or the black Dr. Martens combat boots I had seen for sale at the thrift store, which happened to be Sadie's size (seven-and-a-half), and which already brandished a Sex Pistols sticker on the toe of the left boot. Or (and this was my favorite) the suitcase victrola that I had inherited from my grandfather, which, once accompanied by a half-dozen punk records, would communicate to Sadie unequivocally, "This thing we have should last forever."

Except that, on the morning I broached the topic, Sadie expressed pure revulsion.

"Commodified affection," she said and pretended to vomit on my shoes. "Gross."

"Even still," I said. "You're my girlfriend, and I'd like to give you something."

She smiled when I said this, and I could see that it was the smile of someone riding the aftermath of a low-level epiphany. She straddled me, kissed my neck, then my lips, then my ears, where she whispered, "I know something you could give me. It would be the best gift ever."

She continued kissing me, and I asked, "What is it?" at which point she reached into the pocket of her leather jacket and removed a tube of black lipstick. She used the lipstick to write her name across the top of my hand. She wrote it in large, thick letters, more slashed than scripted.

"Give me this," she said, nodding at my hand. "Only permanent."

"A tattoo?"

"Yes."

"Of your name?"

"Yes."

"But that would be—"

"Forever," she said. "Exactly."

Poomph (from me to Sadie):
"I love you. I am the milkman of human kindness." Beneath this: *"Billy Bragg."*

Poomph (from Sadie to me):
"Someday, I'll feel no pain. Someday, I won't have a brain. They'll take away the part that hurts, and let the rest remain." Beneath this: *"Black Flag."*

I asked my mother what she would say if I came home with a tattoo. She laughed then said, "You're the writer. Imagine the worst."

I asked Coach Mac for his take on tattoos, since he had several on his forearm, including one that reminded me of a Homer Winslow painting with its small red boat about to be capsized by a large gray wave. Coach said, "You remember what I told you about adverbs?" He had said that adverbs should not be used unless the sentence absolutely required their presence. He said, "It's the same with tattoos."

Me: Any update on the rent situation?
  Sadie: Yeah, dummy. They're raising it.
  Me: Is your mom going to be able to pay it?
  Sadie: No. She can't pay the current rent.
  Me: Well what's the plan?
  Sadie: Do we look like plan people to you?

"Have you thought about giving your life to Christ?" This was my mother. Same place, different night.
  "I have," I said.

"And?"

"I'm still thinking."

You should know about Limey. Limey was a guy who lived in Sadie's trailer park. According to Sadie, he was a genius in the realm of tattoos.

"Is that what he does?" I said. "Professionally, I mean."

"No," she said. "It's something he learned in prison. But don't worry. He's good. He gave my mom this one that looks like kudzu, and it wraps all the way from her wrist to her shoulder."

"He sounds very talented."

"So you're game?"

"I'm thinking about it."

"What a way to die," she said. "*Thinking*."

My father (on the phone one night): I have good news and bad news. Which do you want first?

Me: The bad news. You should always lead with the bad news.

My father: Okay, here it is. I'm moving. I met someone, and it's been serious for a while, and I'm moving to Arizona to be close.

Me: You met someone?

My father: Her name is Tanya. I'll tell you, son,
　　　　 this internet thing is wild. I never thought
　　　　 I'd fall in love on the computer, but hey,
　　　　 it's a brave new world, isn't it?

Me: Does Mom know?

My father: Of course. She's known since this past
　　　　 summer, and she's supportive. And you
　　　　 should know that I plan on coming up here
　　　　 a couple times a month.

Me: Well that's good.

My father: I'll be down there for Christmas, but
　　　　 I'll be back up here for New Year's.

Me: Okay.

My father: Aren't you going to ask?

Me: Ask what?

My father: What the good news is.

Me: What's your good news, Dad?

My father: Tanya is pregnant! You're going to be
　　　　 a big brother!

After talking to my father on the phone, I found my
mother in the garage, more staring at the canned
vegetables than sorting them. When she saw me, she
walked over and wrapped me in a hug. I asked her if
she was okay, and she said she was, though we both

knew it was a lie. She asked me if I was okay, and I told her I was, though we both knew it was a cover.

"People can do such weird things," she said.

"Because they think the end is near?" I said.

"No," she said. "Because they're people."

I had a dream that night about being in Arizona and meeting my baby brother. He had a lemon for a head, and at some point, my dad introduced me to Tanya, who looked like Carmen Electra, only red-eyed and covered with crocodile scales. The three of us strolled through a desert and took turns holding my citrus-headed brother. Coach Mac once said, "Tell a dream, lose a reader," but this one feels useful.

The next day at school, I told Sadie about my dad leaving. She punched me in the chest and said, "How does it feel?"

"It hurts," I said. "But strangely enough, it also feels inevitable."

"*Inevitable*," she said. "Now we're talking."

She punched me again, this time in the stomach, and was about to walk away when I pulled her back and said, "Take me to Limey. I'm ready."

Here is a picture of my tattoo. Notice that the thick, black font resembles Sadie's actual handwriting. Notice also that the E at the end has been rendered as a bomb. That was Limey's idea. It didn't hurt like I thought it would hurt, and Sadie was there the entire time. She was holding me from behind and whispering in my ear, "Don't die. Don't die. Don't die."

The reactions to my tattoo were not what I expected. Instead of crying, my mother shrugged and said, "I give up." Instead of making a joke, my father seemed genuinely furious when he said, "Why the hell did you get it on your hand? Now everyone who sees you is going to think you're a dumbass." And when Miss Meechum saw it the next day in class, she pointed to the bomb and said, "At least that part's a nice touch." I have catalogued these reactions here for the sake of the assignment, but if you are wondering exactly how much shame was generated by their disapproval, the answer is none. It felt good to treat my body like a capsule and mark it with a word I believed in.

Billy Beale learned a new word: masochist.

"I told my mom about your tattoo," he said. "She said you were a masochist."

"What's a masochist?"

"Someone who likes to be hurt better than they like being loved."

"Okay," I said. "I'm a masochist. I'm glad we got that settled."

I asked Sadie what she thought about the tattoo.

"I love it," she said.

I asked her why. I had expected her to say, "Because it means you won't forget me," or "Because it'll remind you of all the great memories we've made." But those were my words, and never once in the time we were together did Sadie use anything close to my words.

"I love it," she said. "Because you weren't supposed to do it."

"Look what we do to each other. Look what we do to ourselves. Everyone's a masochist." Coach Mac.

"Do you think this thing with Tanya feels good because you're not supposed to do it?"

This is what I said to my father, after I had several

days to process the fact that he was moving to Arizona to start a new family.

I could tell from the sound of his voice that this question hurt him, which was more or less my intention. There was a punch I had been waiting to throw ever since he announced his plan. I wanted him to walk right into it, and he did. He said, "What is it that you think I'm supposed to do?"

"Come home. Love Mom."

One night, when there was nothing better to do, I eavesdropped on a conversation between my parents. Lucky for me, it was about Sadie.

"What I'm about to say isn't Christ-like," my mother said. "But that girl is white trash. I saw them the other day in that pipe. The leather, the cigarettes, the language—what does Junah see in her?"

"She has moxie," my father said. "You have to give her that."

"That hair," she said. "Those boots."

"Maybe he has a thing for boots. Some folks do."

I heard my mother sigh, and I heard my father mute his television.

"Tell me it's a phase he's going through."

"It's a phase he's going through."

"Tell me we didn't fail as parents."

"We didn't fail as parents."

They were quiet for a long time after this. They were so quiet for so long I decided to hang up and go back to bed. As I was putting down the receiver, I heard one last thing.

"What then?" my mother said. "Let them be?"

"You know how it works," my father said. "We love how we can."

Here is a picture of Tanya. As you can tell from the modest bob and the olive blouse, she appears to be a respectable woman. Nothing close to a red-eyed, scaly Carmen Electra. She works as a financial advisor, and in her free time, she enjoys going to farmer's markets, reading historical romance novels, and going on long walks in the evening with Deuce, her golden retriever. I'm told she has already chosen a name for my brother. *Emerson*. It is hard (but not impossible) to loathe well-composed strangers.

Everyone else had one capsule. I was up to thirteen. Some of mine weren't even shoeboxes. One was an old aquarium. Another was my father's old duffel bag.

"That's against the rules," said a boy from my class.

"Is it?" I said. "That explains why I'm so happy."

The tattoo played a trick on my mind (or was it my eyes?). Whereas before I got it, it was hard to imagine having a single word on my body, now it was the inverse. Now every inch of uninked skin looked sad and incomplete. It wasn't enough that Sadie's name was on my hand. I wanted everything—my fingers and my wrists and my forearms and my shoulders—to play host to their own collection of words and images and colors. I wanted to look down at my body and see a clutter of strange and lovely things. This, as you have gathered by now, is my problem—I am easily moved by new mediums.

I stayed up most of the night thinking up ideas for new tattoos. This meant I fell asleep in Miss Meechum's class. Sadie saved me with a paper ball that struck directly between my eyes. I flattened it and read, "*I cut in line. I bled to death. I got to you. There was nothing left.*" Beneath this: "*Jawbreaker.*"

Sadie gave me time and music and enough memories to fill a thousand shoeboxes. What she didn't give me (what she refused, on principle, to give anyone) was her past. Take the day we passed a stray lab, and I asked her if she had ever owned a dog.

"Knowledge is power," she said in a voice she reserved for quoting one of her punk DVDs. "The more someone knows about you, the more power they have over you."

"I understand," I said. "But I don't want power over you. I just want to know if you ever had a dog."

"No."

"No, you didn't have a dog?"

"No, I'm not going to answer your question."

I said, "It's hard to connect with someone who won't tell you anything about their past."

She said, "That's the idea."

I wanted to believe that two people could build a connection and that when attempting to build one, words were the best tools available. But the evidence was not encouraging. Here is a boy and a girl, both born and raised in my hometown, attempting dialogue in the cafeteria.

"I'm starting to suspect that males are born with an appetite for violence," the boy said. "I crushed a beetle this morning for no reason at all. Saw him crossing the sidewalk like an innocent creature on his way to do some beetle business. Then—*boom!*—I smashed him. Why, though? What was the point?"

"What are you implying about females?" the girl, who was blowing tiny pink bubbles with her gum, responded. "That we're weak?"

"No," the boy said. "I'm not talking about girls at all."

"And why not?" said the girl. "You never talk about girls, unless it's about what girls you want to date. What does that say about your outlook?"

"Let me try again," the boy said. "I walk around with a readiness to hurt things. Sometimes this readiness extends to people. I have a good life, yet I want to cause damage. Why is that?"

"So you're saying that boys shouldn't be held responsible for being violent assholes?"

At this, the boy got up and moved to another table. Someone asked the girl what happened. She popped the biggest pink bubble I had ever seen and replied, "What a little fascist."

Me: Seriously, though, it's not like I'm asking about
    your deepest regret or darkest fear. I just want
    to know if you've ever had a dog.
Sadie: Seriously—no.

There was a small group of Lutherans at my school who held prayer meetings in the morning, at lunch, and at the bus stop.

"Would you like to join us?" asked one of the Christians, a chubby, blue-eyed kid who killed you with his indiscriminate kindness.

"No," I said. "But can you say a prayer for me anyway?"

"How are you doing with the end of the world? Are you anxious?"

"No," I said. "I try not to think about it."

He pulled out a little notebook, which contained a column of names and prayer requests. Still smiling, he said, "Then how can we pray for you?"

"Connection," I said. "I have some, but I'd like more."

"Anything else?" he said.

"Yeah," I said. "Pray for snow."

Late December meant rumors of snow, a minor miracle this far south. It meant falling asleep under the echo of the confident voices of local weathermen, all of whom brandished bad haircuts and looked vaguely alcoholic: "As you can see, this cold front is going to come down from North Carolina and leave us with a nice little dusting. Nothing as of now, but expect two to three inches of snow in the morning." It meant waking up and looking out your window to where the same green grass and the same gray pavement laughed in the face of your capacity for hope.

We kept waiting for snow. Even though most days it was seventy-four degrees, and everyone was wearing short sleeves, and most of the trees had most of their leaves. We looked at the Christmas decorations, those great lights and goofy plastics, and we told ourselves snow was what was supposed to happen. You can wait for anything if you have been convinced of its inevitability.

Here is a note that was deposited into one of my capsules without my knowledge:

Fuck you and your greed for the past. You wanted to know if I ever had a dog. I didn't, and here is why.

When I was six, we lived in Florida, and my dad was staying with us, and we had a place in this shitty trailer park right on the water where your backyard was swamp, and where you couldn't go anywhere without seeing frogs and turtles and sometimes even gators.

One time I caught this little frog, and I made a house for him out of a shoebox. I came into the trailer holding the shoebox. I was on my way to the kitchen to look for something that could be a frog bathtub. Mom wasn't home. Dad was sitting in his chair. He was doing what he did best, which was drink beer and watch television.

One minute I was walking, thinking about that bathtub. Next, I was flying.

Dad kicked me so hard it lifted me off the ground. My head left a hole in the drywall. The shoebox was flattened beneath my legs. And when I stood up, the place where his boot had struck me felt on fire with pain. I stood up and looked inside the box.

I said, "Freddy?"

The frog was motionless, but I picked him up anyway, and I rubbed his stomach. I squeezed him in the place I thought his heart would be. When he didn't move, I put the lid back on the shoebox and started toward my room. Dad was still in his chair. He was laughing.

"You want to know what that was for?" he said.

"What?" I said.

"That was for nothing," he said.

He leaned forward after saying that. He leveled his watery eyes at me and said, "Now if that was for nothing, imagine what the world's gonna do when you actually mess up."

I put the box in the trash and went to my room. I was almost there when he said, "And who the hell is Freddy?"

I never told him it was the name I gave to the frog, and I never told my mother what happened, but now that I've told you, you will think that you know something about me. Except you don't, and you can't, which is why I put this in the capsule with the rest of your sad trivialities.

Poomph (from me to Sadie):
I'm sorry about that stuff with your dad.

Poomph (from Sadie to me):
I don't know what you're talking about.

Coach Mac caught me doodling in class. I had drawn a frog wearing a Ramones T-shirt. I had put a guitar in one of his hands and a cigarette in his mouth. All this under the heading "Ideas for New Tattoo."

"Adverbs," Coach said. "Remember that. They're like adverbs."

Here is the last thing Miss Meechum ever said to our class: "Say hi if you see me in the supermarket." She said this during the last class of the last day before Christmas break, after confirming that the rumors were true—she had been fired, not only for the assignment but for what she described as "a general unwillingness to comply." Miss Meechum said that she had loved teaching us, and that she hoped we would continue the assignment, even though it would no longer count toward our official grade.

"The thing is," she said (now crying). "This place is broken, but it still deserves a story."

Then she said that thing about the supermarket, and the girls in the class began to cry, and a couple of the boys cried too, and it seemed like Miss Meechum wanted to say more, but before she could, the bell rang, and everyone hugged her and ran out of the room the way that you run when Christmas break has officially begun. Only I stayed behind.

Here is the last thing Miss Meechum ever said to me: "How many capsules do you have now?"

"Seventeen."

"Keep going," she said. "You're almost there."

After school that day, I tried to find Coach Mac. I wanted to ask him if he knew anything about Miss Meechum's replacement. But Coach wasn't in his classroom, and he wasn't in the faculty lounge. On my way out, I passed the roof where Coach would drink his beer and lift his weights. Sure enough: I could hear him up there. I called his name, but he did not respond. I called it again, and still nothing. Eventually, I picked up a rock and threw it toward where I imagined he was. That did it.

"It's over!" he shouted. "Go home!"

First day of break, and finally it snowed. The trees, the streets, the houses: everything quiet and white and looking like it could stay that way forever. Sadie and I met at The Pipe, where even under the winter coats and shared quilt, we could not stop shaking. We didn't mind the shaking. We felt more alone than ever.

We were alone until Thick-neck—a boy who would go on to run the third most successful barbeque chain in the state of South Carolina—ducked into The Pipe for no apparent reason other than to chew an icicle. Clamping the icicle like a cigar, he looked at Sadie and I huddled together under our blanket, and he grunted, "Fucking weirdos."

My response was to look at Sadie, and when I did, she was smiling as if she had just received a test back and the grade was very high. I smiled the same smile, and we laughed as the boy wandered off through the woods. Then she put her arm around me and kissed me on the mouth. The snow was falling so slowly outside, and I could not feel my face, and I thought to myself, "If it has to end, let it end like this."

Coach was right about adverbs. And yet, adverbs are not without utility. They are good for describing how things happen.

Suddenly.

The first night of Christmas break, Sadie called our house. She called past midnight, and my mother answered the phone and, although I could not hear what Sadie was saying, I did hear my mother ask her, "Is everything okay over there?" Then a long pause. Then my mother (sighing): "Sweetheart, are you sure?"

When I got on the line, I could hardly hear Sadie over the background noise. There were sounds I could identify. Mainly: Sadie's mom screaming; the angry voice of a man screaming back; also music being played at a blistering volume; and someone honking a car horn repeatedly. But these sounds were blended with other violent noises that (to my ear) were entirely alien: some kind high-pitched wailing that could've been human or electronic; a repeated (and nearly rhythmic) slamming; and a vicious crunching sound as if someone was running a scouring pad over the phone's mouthpiece. Through all of this, I barely heard Sadie when she said, "Two things. Then I gotta go."

I tried to stop her. Twice, I said, "Hold on. Are you okay?" But Sadie kept talking, either because she could not hear me, or because she was running out of time.

"First," she said. "Thank you. For being my friend, I mean. I had never done that before."

I could hear Sadie palm the mouthpiece, a gesture which muffled (though not by much) the sound of her mom scream, "Say I won't do it! Say I won't do it! I swear to God I will!"

"Sadie!" I screamed. "What is happening?"

There was no response. Just more noise, including a complete stop to the high-pitched wailing and a drastic increase in the scour pad scratching. I heard the man, angry and seemingly drunk, say, "I'm not going anywhere."

"The second thing," Sadie said. "And I have to make this quick."

This was the moment when I realized what was happening. That Sadie was saying goodbye, and that she had been saying goodbye for sometime, and that not only was I powerless to stop her from leaving, but that she didn't want to be stopped from leaving. My throat locked up, and I started grasping for words that weren't there. I said the only thing that I could think to say, and that was, "Wait, wait, wait."

"The second thing I want to say is—"

"Sadie, wait. I'm coming over. I'll be there in five minutes."

"The second thing—"

Then came the loudest noise of all: a crash accompanied by the breaking of glass. There was the man's voice screaming, "I told you not to touch me!" There was Sadie's mom screaming, "Get off the phone!" There was the return of the high-pitched wailing, and then Sadie, one last time: "Shit. He's got a gun. I gotta go."

Once.

Here is my favorite picture of Sadie. It was taken at the stairwell at school, where, this one time, Sadie and I snuck out of the cafeteria, so that she could play her guitar. She is smiling in this photograph, though a minute before taking it, a group of football players passed by, one of whom said, "You sound like garbage." I don't need to tell you what she did in response. You already know that her smile did not change, and that she played her song louder, until the football players were gone, and we were alone again.

Inevitably.

I had a dream that Sadie's phone call was a dream. We were in The Pipe, and it was snowing, and I told her that I had a nightmare where we said goodbye over the telephone. We were huddled under some blankets, and she brought my tattoo to her lips. She kissed each letter of her name and said, "Nice try, but you're stuck with me."

I woke up, I got dressed, and I walked to Sadie's trailer, where I found what I knew I would find. It was empty, and her mother's car was gone. It was clear that no one lived here anymore, but because I held out for some hidden theory that operates outside of where observable facts of reality begin and end, I walked down to the office and talked to the manager.

"They left in the night," she said. "No notice, no rent."

I started to walk away when the manager asked me, "Was she a friend of yours?"

I said what I could, which was nothing. Then I walked on through the cold morning. There was snow on the ground, and I couldn't feel my fingers. My breath went ahead of me in tiny puffs of smoke. What I needed was a fire.

Old habits: I made a cave of blankets in my room and stayed inside straight through Christmas. I read a little, and I ate a little, and I fooled with my capsules a little, but mostly I lay there and listened to *London Calling* on repeat. Mostly I waited for my mother to come in and say, "Junah, there's a phone call for you." Joe Strummer sang, "The ice age is coming." I believed him.

My mother told my father about Sadie. He called me from Arizona to see how I was doing.

My father: How does it feel?

Me: It hurts.

My father: Come on, cave dweller. You can do
        better than that.

Me: It feels like something inside me died. A
        dream. Or maybe just an idea. But it was
        there, and I relied on it, and now it's gone.

My father: That's a little better.
Me: Tell me it comes back in time.
My father: No.
Me: Why not?
My father: Because it doesn't. This one is gone,
          pal. All the way gone.

Included here is a catalogue of well-intentioned truisms offered to me after Sadie's departure:
    "Everything happens for a reason."
    "You're better off without her."
    "There are plenty of fish in the sea."
    "Time heals all wounds."
    "Her loss."
You'll notice that I've placed these beside a brand-new lighter. To make it easier for you, I've soaked the list in a highly flammable liquid. Kill every word that isn't true.

I can't talk about Christmas morning. I have pretended thus far to be clear-eyed, but some things are too sad for reportage. Take this omission as an opportunity to insert something magical. Say I opened presents and watched old movies with my mother. Say she was happy and didn't think about the end.

I will say this: it snowed on Christmas, which is something that had never happened in my lifetime. Like the rest of our town, when the first flakes began to fall, we rushed to the supermarket for bread, milk, and batteries. I saw Miss Meechum in the bread aisle, and I ran up to her. I wanted to tell her about Sadie, but I also had some questions about the assignment. It was thrilling to see her like this, but when I tapped her on the shoulder, the woman who turned around was not Miss Meechum. It was a tired-looking mother, angry too, who scoffed and said, "Do I know you?"

December 28th, December 29th, and December 30th: three days, three postcards. All three cards were from Okeechobee, Florida. None of them had a return address.

Here is the first one. On the side meant for text, there are four crude drawings arranged in panels like a comic strip. Panel one: a girl holds in her hand a bulbous cartoon heart, while above her head a thought bubble contains the words I'M HUNGRY! Panel two: the girl (now smiling) eats the heart (now bleeding). Panel three: the girl squats down and shits out a small pile of heart-shards. Panel four: the girl (now pensive) looks out of her frame and directly at the reader. The speech bubble in this fourth and final frame reads, *I'M STILL HUNGRY!*

"Is that from Sadie?" my mother asked, having seen me studying the postcard for several hours.

"No," I said. "It's from Florida."

Here is the second postcard. Like the first, it has no return address and no information that would identify its sender. Also like the first, it features original artwork—a single panel where an old man with a beard is conversing with a large, black bomb. "God" is written under the old man, and "December 31st" is written under the bomb. The old man says to the bomb, "What are you doing?" The bomb says back, "Killing time."

If you look closely at the third frame on the first postcard, the one in which the girl shits out the heart, you can see that, if rearranged correctly, all the little heart-shards would actually cohere their original form. The geometry works out perfectly. There are no missing pieces, and there are no extra pieces. Put aside your craving for palatable people and themes. You have to admire an artist who attends to the details.

Consider the third and final postcard. This one featured a cartoon Elvis (old and puffy, not young and handsome). Elvis was sitting on the toilet, his head thrown back in agony, his hands clutching his heart. He was dying; and yet, he was singing. He was wailing, "Time goes by so slowly. And time can do so much. Are you still mine?"

Because I refused to lie, and because she refused to coerce, my mother and I finished our year of conversations about God at an impasse. Take this conversation, which took place on the night of December 30th, about half a minute before I crossed over into the realm of sleep.

My mother: Say that you believe in Jesus.

Me: I believe in Jesus.

My mother: Do you mean that?

Me: I could say that I mean it.

My mother: I think I've failed you.

Me: That's absurd. You're the best mom ever.

My mother: And yet, you don't believe.
Me: I could say I do. If it makes you happy, I
      could say anything at all.

I have included the Gospel of Mark here, since the
closest I came to embracing my mother's faith was
in reading the life of Christ. Three years of healing
the sick and helping the poor, only to be abandoned
by your friends, spit on by the world, and nailed to
a cross where you ask the One you love, "Why have
You forsaken me?" In the realm of smashed hearts, it
gets no lower than Christ. Was I a believer? I never
knew. But Christ was a beautiful, ancient madman,
and when I read about His death and resurrection,
I felt that, if I were to kill time with Someone, this
would be my guy.

My dad got into town on the morning of December
31st. He was tan, and he had a beard, but otherwise,
he looked about the same. He told me the day was
mine, and I told him I had twenty-three capsules,
not counting yours, that needed burying. I told him I
didn't want to talk about Y2K (because there wasn't
anything interesting left to say on the subject), and I

told him I didn't want to talk about Sadie (because, there too, the conversation was beginning to feel redundant).

"I have some Arizona stories," he said. "Want to hear those?"

"Let's go."

We went. To various old mills and abandoned factories; to fishing ponds and baseball fields; to a construction site; to a junkyard; to a cemetery; to the blackberry patch behind the house where he grew up; to the magnolia tree in front of the house where my mother grew up; to seven different churches of seven different denominations; and finally to the dried-up creek bed behind The Pipe. We drove all over town, and we buried all the capsules, and we came home tired and talked out, ready to sit in front of a television and watch the new year bring itself in.

We were parked in the driveway when he said, "Just between you and me, are you curious about what's going to happen tonight?"

"Of course. Who isn't curious?"

"Let me ask you something. If they turned out to be right, if tonight really was the end, is there anything you'd regret?"

"Sure."

"Such as?"

"I wish you and Mom had found a way to stay together."

"Yeah, I'd die with that one too."

"Did you get them all in the ground?" my mother asked.

"All but one," I said. I meant you.

"Why the one?"

"Because it needs more."

"More what?"

"More everything."

Here is the last conversation of the century. It happened in the living room of a small house in upstate South Carolina, on a couch and just before midnight. Here I am, tired from digging and struggling to keep my eyes open. Here are my mother and my father, and though they are no longer together, they are holding each other and talking about the new year. Here is how it happened, as best as I remember.

My mother: Wake up, Junah. It's almost midnight.

My father: Let him sleep.

My mother: How could we? If something happens, he needs to see it.

My father: Nothing is going to happen.

My mother: It could.

My father: That's true. But it won't.

My mother: You shouldn't be so certain. It's not
good for your heart.

My father: Look! The bomb!

My mother: Wake up, Honey. They're about to
drop the bomb.

Me: The bomb?

My mother: What? No—the *ball*. Wake up.

I opened my eyes and watched a giant ball of light descend toward a crowd of people huddled together in the dark, some of whom looked happy, some of whom looked scared. I could not decide how I felt, or even what I was expected to feel, mainly because I did not know what the light was supposed to signify when it hit the ground—a world about to end, or a world hardly begun. It was because I did not know that I looked even harder.

Acknowledgments

Thanks to Jason Howard and the editors at *Appalachian Review*, who published this book's opening chapter and consequently encouraged its completion. Thanks to the bottomlessly wonderful folks at Hub City: Meg Reid, Kate McMullen, and Julie Jarema. Thanks to brilliant teachers: Dean Bakopoulos, Nic Brown, Matt Hooley, Allegra Hyde, T. Geronimo Johnson, Keith Morris, Lee Morrissey, Ron Rash, George Singleton, David Shields, and Debra Spark. Thanks to inestimable friends: Michael Bible, Megan "Sarge" Busch, Phil Canipe, Scott Gould, Stephen Hundley, Cole Jeffrey, Denton Loving, Matt Meade, Matt Merson, Mark Richard, Nic Richardson, Titus Staples, and Aaron Straumwasser. Thanks to Greenville people: Pat, Lydia, Ashley, Matt, Jenny, Nathan, Ally, and Omie. Thanks finally to Hannah, whose love has always felt like its own kind of apocalypse.

About the Author

Winner of *Texas Review's* Southern Poetry Breakthrough Award, Dan Leach is the author of *Floods and Fires, Dead Mediums,* and *Stray Latitudes.* He lives in the lowcountry of South Carolina and teaches writing at Charleston Southern University.

PUBLISHING
New & Extraordinary
VOICES FROM THE
AMERICAN SOUTH

Celebrating its 30th year in 2025, Hub City Press has emerged as the South's premier independent literary press. Founded in Spartanburg, South Carolina in 1995, Hub City is interested in books with a strong sense of place and is committed to finding and spotlighting extraordinary new and unsung writers from the American South. Our curated list champions diverse authors and books that don't fit into the commercial or academic publishing landscape.

THE SOUTH CAROLINA NOVEL SERIES is open to all writers in South Carolina. It is co-sponsored by the South Carolina Arts Commission, the South Carolina State Library, and South Carolina Humanities.

PREVIOUS WINNERS
2023: Robert Maynor   *The Big Game is Every Night*
2021: Maris Lawyer   *The Blue Line Down*
2019: Scott Sharpe   *A Wild Eden*
2017: Brock Adams   *Ember*
2015: James McTeer   *Minnow*

HUB CITY PRESS books are made possible through the generous support of grants and donations from corporations, state and federal grant programs, family foundations, and the many individuals who support our mission of building a more inclusive literary arts culture, in particular: Byron Morris, Charles and Katherine Frazier, and Michel and Eliot Stone. Hub City Press gratefully acknowledges support from the National Endowment for the Arts, the Amazon Literary Partnership, the South Carolina Arts Commission, Spartanburg County Public Library, and the City of Spartanburg.

Sabon LT Pro
10.8/16.2